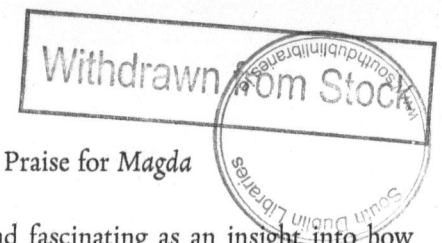

Praise for *Magda*

'Challenging, clever, and fascinating as an insight into how generations of Germans are summoning the courage to address the horror of the last century.' —AMANDA CRAIG

'A book which does that is one we should all be reading, so find a copy. It has been one of my reading experiences of the year.' —SIMON SAVIDGE

OBSERVER BOOKS OF THE YEAR 'This is an intelligent, acute and horrifically intense book. It didn't so much take my breath away as make me gasp for air.' —SAM JORDISON

Praise for *Clara's Daughter*

'The deftly arranged sequence of scenes gradually reveals the fears and needs of each protagonist and their relationships with each other, outlined with a careful, thoughtful style that creates an unusual atmosphere of charged bleakness. Strange, but oddly impressive.' —HARRY RITCHIE, *Daily Mail*

'This searching, beautifully written novel gets to the heart of woman's attempts to step out of the role of her mother's daughter, and make sense of the person she has become. Terrific.' —KATE SAUNDERS, *The Times*

Praise for *Kauthar*

'*Kauthar*, as much an exploration of breakdown and collapse as of the lines between devotion and delusion, faith and fundamentalism, does not shy away from suffering and darkness; instead, as in *Magda* and *Clara's Daughter*, Ziervogel goes bravely to the bleakest points of humanity and illuminates them with her lyrical and enthralling prose.' —CLAIRE KOHDA HAZELTON, *The Guardian*

'Ziervogel writes with insight and fluency, articulating a profound empathy with those at the extreme reaches of their endurance. Searingly contemporary, *Kauthar* sketches out a humane and subtle counterpoint to the distorted debate surrounding religious radicalisation, and in doing so is resonant and timely.' —LETTIE KENNEDY, *The Observer*

Praise for *The Photographer*

'Two generations on from her own Grandmother's experience, Ziervogel shines a humanising light into the dark spots of her country's history.' —LUCY ASH, *The Observer*

'Few books have the ability to move the reader in the first pages, as *The Photographer* does . . . Ziervogel makes us question ideas of innocence and blame during fraught times . . . Meike Ziervogel shows us the less visible effects of war, and the ways in which it can corrupt and change us.' —CLAIRE KOHDA HAZELTON, *Times Literary Supplement*

FLOTSAM

MEIKE ZIERVOGEL grew up in Germany and came to Britain in 1986 to study Arabic. In 2008, she founded Peirene Press. *Flotsam* is Meike's fifth novel. Find out more about Meike at www.meikeziervogel.com

Also by Meike Ziervogel

Magda
Clara's Daughter
Kauthar
The Photographer

FLOTSAM

MEIKE ZIERVOGEL

SALT

CROMER

PUBLISHED BY SALT PUBLISHING 2019

2 4 6 8 10 9 7 5 3 1

First published in Great Britain in 2019 by
Salt Publishing Ltd
12 Norwich Road, Cromer NR27 0AX United Kingdom

www.saltpublishing.com

Salt Publishing Limited Reg. No. 5293401

A CIP catalogue record for this book is available from the British Library

ISBN 978 1 78463 178 9 (Paperback edition)
ISBN 978 1 78463 179 6 (Electronic edition)

Typeset in Neacademia by Salt Publishing

Printed and bound in Great Britain by Clays Ltd, Elcograf S.p.A

MIX
Paper from responsible sources
FSC® C018072
FSC www.fsc.org

Salt Publishing Limited is committed to responsible forest management.
This book is made from Forest Stewardship Council™ certified paper.

FLOTSAM

TRINE

TRINE CLIMBS DOWN from the shipwreck. She moves swiftly. Swift like the wind that is blowing in from the sea. Her brother is lying on the sand. Dead. She knows it before she gets to him.

She had reached out to him. Said, 'Quick, quick, they are coming. Give me your hand.'

No one was coming. They were playing. She was playing. Carl looked up and stepped between two rungs of the rope ladder, then lost his balance. And if Trine had leaned further forward she might have been able to grab him. But she didn't. She didn't.

From the corner of her eye the girl can see across the wide expanse of the mudflats. There is a stick figure walking along the dark line of eelgrass that was left behind by the last high tide. Trine's mother often walks for hours along the shore, collecting driftwood and flotsam and jetsam. The smaller pieces, such as bottles and tins and toys and shoes, she puts in a rucksack. The bigger pieces, such as wooden planks and boxes, she places in a handcart which she usually pulls along behind her. But today she's carrying only the rucksack.

Trine's now next to her brother. The wind is whistling in the girl's ears, pulling her hair back, tearing at her cardigan. Carl looks totally normal – Trine kneels down and puts her ears to his chest – except that his chest isn't moving. She strokes his head. She feels sorry that he is dead. For him she feels sorry. He loved playing on the shipwreck, pretending they were out on the high seas, where they would attack the vessels of evil merchants, robbing them of their goods and then giving everything to the poor. Like Klaus Störtebeker, the famous pirate, who had never been afraid of the sea or the wind or the depth of the water. While Carl was. Oh yes, he was. He had never even learned to swim. Still, he would have loved to be as brave and courageous as Störtebeker. And now he won't ever again have that chance.

But Trine won't run to her mother. Her mother won't help. Her mother can't sort it out. Can't sort anything out.

Trine's mother – her name is Anna – spends days, weeks, months fantasizing about being a seamstress, because then she could make clothes. Or a knitter, so she could knit jumpers and cushion covers and blankets. Or a potter who makes mugs and plates and bowls. Or a painter – Anna used to be a painter a long time ago, before Trine was born – who paints pictures that people can look at with horror or delight or maybe indifference. Or even a writer, then at least by the end of it she would have a story. But because Trine's mother relies on what she finds on the beach, washed up by the tide as dictated by the moon and the stars, she might find an old threadbare shirt, but it's never enough to turn into a garment anyone would want – except she, Trine's mother, herself.

Or she might find, as she once did, a hand-knitted scarf, the wool of course matted and felted. She washed it and succeeded in untangling the yarn. Up to a point, because it ripped frequently. Anna used it to make a beautiful woollen flower that she glued onto cardboard. She hung it above Trine's bed. But Carl said it was ugly. So now it hangs in Anna's shed.

Trine's glance travels along the side of the shipwreck. It's three times her height. She needs to get her brother back onboard. Whenever the captain of a pirate ship died, he didn't receive a common sea burial. Instead his corpse was laid out on deck and the crew would disembark before setting fire to the ship. The idea of fire appeals to the girl. (Although it won't appeal to her mother. Trine knows that her mother will be upset when she sees the wreck go up in flames.) Trine likes the thought that the body will burn and escape as smoke up into the air, flying away with the Arctic terns that have already started to set off for their winter quarters.

'You'd like that, wouldn't you?' Trine whispers to her brother. Naturally, no answer. But she knows he would.

On the other hand, to bury him doesn't seem right at all. They once buried a dead seagull. They used an old cardboard box as a coffin, then dug a hole and afterwards filled it with earth. In the evening in bed Trine suddenly couldn't breathe, because she imagined that the gull might wake up again, discovering that it was imprisoned in a pitch-black box. It would flap its wings, trying to get out, trying to fly away, and find it couldn't. And then it would die very slowly, suffocating. Trine started to cry and eventually Carl woke up. Together, they sneaked out in the middle of the night with a torch to rescue the seagull from the hole and the box. Trine carried the bird in her cupped hands and hid it under her bed. The next day she put it in her satchel, wrapped in paper. On her way to school she left it under a bush. She didn't know what else to do. She didn't want to take it with her to school because someone – Hauke or Jens or Norbert – might have found the bird and torn out its feathers and ripped off its wings and head. She felt bad, a coward, that she had left the dead seagull under the bush. A cat might find it, or a dog. As Trine cycled home from school that day she spotted the empty package out of the corner of her eye. She didn't stop. And the next day she went a different way even though it was longer. But at least she could forget – or pretend to forget – that it was her who had left the dead seagull under the bush.

Still, as she is now squatting by her brother's side, she realizes that being eaten by a cat or a dog is better than being buried in a hole. In a hole you can wake up, but once you've been eaten you are gone. Not flying off into the endless skies with the Arctic terns. But still gone.

The girl rocks gently back and forth with her elbows resting on her knees. 'Don't worry, Carl. I won't leave you under a bush and I won't bury you in a hole. You will receive a funeral worthy of a great pirate.'

But to succeed, Trine's mother mustn't find out that Carl is dead. She would mess it all up with her tears and her wailing and her accusations. No way. Trine is in no mood to deal with her mother. And her mother would probably insist that her brother needs to be buried. In the churchyard. Next to Dad. Mum loves that sort of stuff. Big drama. At Dad's funeral she turned up all in black with a black veil in front of her face and big black sunglasses. They all had to throw some earth on Dad's coffin. It made Trine cringe, for her father. The noise of the earth spiked with little stones thumping down on the lid. Not only did her father used to be a sea captain who loved the open seas and open skies, he also hated to be disturbed when he was napping. Trine and Carl weren't allowed to make any noise when he had naps at home during the day. No running, no banging of doors, no laughter. They were only allowed to do homework – quietly. Afterwards, after Dad's funeral, there were many days when Mum didn't get out of bed or, when she was out of bed, she cried. And sometimes she raged and smashed things – plates and her most precious vase. Bang, against the wall behind the sofa.

No, thank you. Trine is not keen to see her mother behave that way.

So, for a start it means that she mustn't notice that Carl is gone.

Well, that means Trine has to get Carl back onto the shipwreck as fast as possible.

But how? She won't be able to carry him slung over her shoulder up the ladder.

She needs time to think.

She pulls her brother closer to the wreck. They are now in the lee of the ship, where the wind can't reach them. She takes off her cardigan, folds it and pushes it under her brother's head.

The ship sits on a sandbank that is only ever fully flooded at the very high storm tides that come along once or twice in a lifetime, not more, like the one in the winter of 1945, when the vessel had washed up. Trine is too young to remember, but her father told her. The sandbank is high but not very wide. And only a couple of metres away the mud sizzles and splatters and slurps, and although it looks empty and barren and dead, it's not. The mudflats are teeming with snails and cockles and sandhoppers living just beneath the surface. And these creatures produce the squelching sounds which suddenly begin to hammer inside Trine's head, now that she can no longer hear the wind. Goosebumps spread across her body despite the fact that she's known these noises all her life. But what if this time the noise means something different? What if the mudflats are unhappy that Carl is no longer here? Trine puts her hands over her ears and fixes her gaze on the dry patch just in front of her feet. Between her and Carl's tracks she can make out bird marks. She leans forward. Gulls and geese have webbing between their three toes. Plovers have no webbing at all, while oystercatchers have a big, ugly, rippled middle toe. There! Trine spots one.

'You wouldn't have been quicker finding the oystercatcher among all the mess we've made here today in the sand, would you?' She smiles at Carl and gently strokes the hair out of his face. He always liked being a long-haired pirate.

TRINE LIFTS CARL into the handcart that she fetched from their cottage, which stands just behind the dyke – running there and back in record time. She covers her brother with the cardigan. His back is damp from lying on the ground, so she needs to make sure that he doesn't get any colder. He looks as if he's asleep. That's what she'd say if her mother or anyone else were unexpectedly to walk around the shipwreck. Not that anyone ever comes here. Even though when Trine was on top of the dyke she saw that her mother had started to head home. But from experience the girl knows that there is still time. Yet she suddenly feels worried. It looks odd having her brother asleep in the handcart. He's too big for it. She pulls the cardigan over his face. But now his legs are poking out. She could fetch the old blanket from inside the boat. No. Time is pressing. She needs to get home before her mother, who will only ask stupid questions to which Trine won't know the answers.

The cart with her brother inside is heavier than the girl had anticipated. Trine first tries to push it. But the wheels sink deep into the mud and she struggles to keep her balance, continually slipping and sliding. So she decides to pull it. For a while she makes good progress. She's keeping her eyes on the ground to avoid stepping on slippery seaweed or jellyfish. Each time she puts her feet down firmly, then waits till they have sunk ankle deep into the ooze. There she lets them settle before she pushes off into the next step. She's concentrating hard and when the shrill cack-cack scream falls out of the sky, aiming straight at her, it takes her a moment to react. Only when the coral-red beak appears right in front of her face does she let go of the cart and lift her arms above her head in protection. The cart behind her tips over, and that, more than the attack of the Arctic tern, which has already disappeared again, taking its horrible cack-cack noise with it, upsets the girl. And a couple of silent tears roll down her cheeks as she straightens the cart, scoops Carl up and puts him back inside. Maybe everyone is angry that she didn't reach out her hand for her brother, she thinks, but there is nothing she can do about it now.

Before taking Carl inside, Trine quickly wipes the mud off him. Then comes the most difficult part. She has to carry him up the stairs, slung over her shoulder, as fast as if she weren't carrying any weight. The stairs are old and wooden and make a lot of noise. They creak and sigh and groan. The girl is holding on to the banister, pulling herself up, trying not to be drawn backwards by the weight.

With a sigh of relief she drops Carl onto her bed. Now they are safe. Until tomorrow morning.

Trine kneels down and pulls from underneath the bed the stuff she tends to hide there: her red pirate trousers and white pirate blouse, and a wooden pirate sabre that her father had made for her.

In her ears she hears Carl's laugh ring out: 'And you really believe no evil intruder would find your things underneath the bed? They always look there first. And into cupboards.'

Trine looks at Carl lying on her bed and gives him a little slap across the top of his head, which she always does when he says something silly. Then she sits back on her feet.

'OK, then. I won't hide you underneath my bed. How do you feel about that?'

Carl doesn't reply. He too knows that he needs to be hidden.

Later on, after supper and when it is dark and her mother has said goodnight and Trine is lying in bed, she doesn't at all like the feeling of her brother sleeping underneath her on the cold, hard floor. Her mother played along with the game that Carl is hiding for the rest of the evening and only she, Trine, is allowed to see him and bring him supper and then tuck him up in bed. Trine and Carl often play games like that. But now Trine would love her brother to crawl out from underneath her bed and jump into his own with a loud pirate yell.

A SUDDEN KNOCK at the door.

'Are you up?' Mum's voice through the door. 'It's already past ten o'clock.'

'Yes, yes, we are up. We are just doing something.'

'I'm going to the market in town. Do you want to come? I can drop you at the library.'

Trine jumps out of bed and shuffles over to Carl. He's lying on his side with his face turned towards the wall. Hiding under her bed half the night has exhausted him. She bends over, gently shaking him by his shoulders.

'Carl, do you want to go to the library today?'

She wouldn't mind going. She's finished all her books. She always reads a lot during school holidays.

Not a murmur. Fast asleep. Trine decides to take that as a no. Oh well. She will just have to cycle into town tomorrow. She straightens up, creeps on tiptoes to the door.

'No, not today,' she whispers.

'Why are you whispering?'

'Because Carl was hiding underneath my bed all night and now he's finally in his, pretending to be asleep. He's going to pretend to be asleep all day. And I have to carry him around, he says. So I have an idea, which is what I'm doing at the moment. But I don't want to talk to you about it yet. That's why I'm not letting you in. I don't want Carl to know what I'm planning. It will be a surprise.' She catches her breath: she's spoken fast.

The previous evening, once Trine had heard her mother brush her teeth and go to her room, she put Carl back into his own bed. She felt so sorry for him because the coldness had made him all stiff. She tucked him in snugly and also gave him her own duvet. Then she took the sheet off her bed and covered herself with that. Luckily the next time she checked on Carl, he had warmed up again and was back to normal. She was able to move his arms and pull her thick blue woollen jumper over his head. She took her duvet back. And then she had the idea! What if she rolled him up in the duvets, making sure he was tied like a parcel, then no one – especially not Mum – would be able to tell if he was alive or dead, and Trine could get him back to the wreck and there she would have time to build a pulley. She had thought of the old door lying on the deck: she could use it to make a simple lifting device by throwing a rope across the broken mast that was hanging over the side of the ship. Then she'd fix the rope to the door, put Carl on top of the door and pull him up.

In the middle of the night, Trine sneaked down to the kitchen and fetched the ball of string from the drawer. That was when she locked the door. She didn't want to be disturbed. If Mum barged in unexpectedly and insisted on shaking Carl awake, not only she, Trine, but also Carl would have been mightily upset with her for destroying the game. And Carl would have then been in a bad mood for the rest of the day.

As Trine now pulls her brother from the bed she tries to avoid any noise. But he's made himself incredibly heavy and his legs thump down on the floor. For a second she halts, waiting for him to complain that it hurts. But no. His eyes remain shut. Not even his face muscles have contorted. He's a good game player, her brother. Trine rolls him into the duvet and ties him up, wrapping the string several times around his body, arms and legs, and a belt loosely around his forehead to stop the duvet slipping away from his face.

'Are you getting enough air?' She's worried that he can't breathe.

She can't tell if he nodded or shook his head. To be on the safe side, she takes the belt away. Bringing him downstairs, she will carry him with his head hanging down so that the duvet won't slip from his face. And once he's in the handcart she might put the belt back on. But anyway, first she has to wait for a couple of hours. High tide is at eleven. By noon it should be fine to get to the sandbank.

TRINE WOULD LIKE her brother to wake up now. The game has gone on far too long. She has built the pulley and pulled Carl up. It took her all afternoon. Luckily her mother never comes down to the mudflats on the days when she goes to town. After coming back she always drinks wine.

The wind has picked up again. Low tide was a couple of hours ago, the water is approaching once again. With it the evening mist is settling in fast and the smell of salt and sludge and slime has got stronger.

Trine looks down at this big duvet sausage now lying on the deck of the wreck. Suddenly she finds the game stupid. A really stupid game. Carl should stop it! Right now!

'Let's go home. I'm hungry,' she says loudly and clearly, so that her brother can hear and will understand that she is serious.

She steps over the duvet, deliberately kicking against it. She doesn't want to hurt Carl. She just wants to make the point. She played along with him all night and the entire day. But now it's enough. She climbs down from the ship, starts walking away, towards the shore, not lifting her feet but instead digging them deep into the mud to produce a lot of squelching noises, so that even from the top of the deck Carl can hear her leaving.

Trine stops, begins to jump on the spot, high and higher, and each time she comes down harder with her feet and more mud splashes up her legs, up her belly and up her chest and even into her face. She wants to kill as many mud snails and sandhoppers and lugworms and whatever else is hiding in the mudflats. Apparently there are a few hundred thousand of these creatures per square metre. Another of those useless pieces of knowledge that Carl has imparted. These creatures are so tiny anyway, they won't notice if they are alive or dead. But Carl will mind. Yes, he will. And maybe that will finally stir him. He even hates stepping on seaweed in the water because he says it's alive.

Eventually Trine turns around and heads back to the shipwreck.

'You are not dead.' She sits on top of the lifejacket box on the deck in front of the cockpit. Her knees pulled up to her chin, arms wrapped around legs, looking at the duvet in front of her. 'You were not dead yesterday. You were not dead last night. And you are not dead now.'

But Carl doesn't move. Instead she hears a feeble *peet-peet* reply from an oystercatcher somewhere above her. She looks up. Wafts of mist move across her vision. For a moment she holds her breath, waiting for the bird's usual trill to follow. But this time nothing. As if the mist has swallowed the sound.

Trine crawls over to her brother and loosens the string that is still holding the duvet around him, then returns to the outer edge of the box.

A creepy feeling now claws its way from her stomach up into her chest. Like the lapping waves of the incoming tide crawling up the sandbank. Maybe it just has to do with the mist that has thickened into fog around her. And the chilly breeze that is stroking over her bare arms and legs as if wanting to mock her, to tease her. Trine can no longer see the shoreline. The dyke has disappeared. The birds have fallen silent. Carl doesn't move. She lies down beside the duvet and puts her arm around her brother. She doesn't want to look at him again.

Unless he wakes up. But she also doesn't want to burn him any longer either. Somehow this idea of his body flying away with the Arctic terns to their winter quarters doesn't sound good any longer. She'd be so lonely. She squeezes him tight.

'Come on, wake up. The game is over. You have won.'

Trine waits, begins to shiver.

She won't let go of him.

Dad had once explained to her how everything around here is made up of different types of sand and that's why the landscape continuously moves and changes and shifts, altered by the coming and going of the currents and waves. Nothing is stable, plants and animals struggle to settle. Only manmade things, such as jetties and dykes and shipwrecks, offer solid ground, a firm base from which colonies of winkles and mussels and barnacles can grow. Where plants and animals are safe from the sea.

Trine buries her nose into where she imagines her brother's shoulder blades to be.

Someone who feels so concrete, so real, just can't be dead.

THE FOG HAS lifted and the rays of the setting sun are breaking through the purple clouds like the long, probing fingers of God. Trine climbs down from the boat. She now has to hurry to make sure she can set it alight before the next high tide. Her mother doesn't like her staying at the wreck as the tide is approaching.

When the girl has reached the top of the dyke she turns around. Squeezing her eyes, focusing hard, she can just about make out the white bundle on the deck of the wreck. But only because she knows it is there.

Carl is dead, Trine, do you hear?

'Carl is dead,' she says out loud to herself. She has to keep it inside her head, but she doesn't like the thought and so it just slips from her mind, again and again and again. She's aware of that happening. She also knows of dead bodies decomposing. After her dad died she read up all about it in the library, of what happens to a dead body. It doesn't of course happen immediately, she still has some time. And the salt in the air slows down the process. Still. She shouldn't put off setting Carl's body on fire and giving him a pirate's burial. She promised him.

She runs down the dyke. Crouching, she scurries closer to the cottage, peeps through the window. Her mother is lying on the sofa. An arm across her eyes, an empty wine glass and a bottle of wine beside her. Her mother only goes to the market once a month. To get what they need. She prefers to be out here with Trine and Carl, and the wind, and the sound of the sea, and the sheep on the dyke and the birds in the sky, she says. Trine turns to the left, where her mother's shed stands.

She carefully opens the door, ready to stop at the first screech. The sun has gone down behind the dyke and inside the shed it's almost completely dark. But she mustn't turn on the light.

Last summer Trine's mother found a beautiful piece of pottery, glazed with a couple of delicate dancers. Maybe a true ancient Greek vase once, maybe an imitation, but the dancers were hand-painted. For a week Anna sat at the bottom of the dyke, on the other side, looking across the Wattenmeer into the setting evening sun, holding the piece in her hand. She hadn't ever worked with clay. But eventually she got a big lump and dug her fingers into it. She loved the squishiness of it, squeezing it through her fingers like the mud under her feet, raising smooth walls, then bending them, moulding them into containers around her hand, her arm. And she wanted to go bigger, she explained to her daughter, she wanted to form a lair around herself. And hide inside, she said. For ever. And that scared her.

Feeling her way, Trine circumnavigates the table in the middle of the shed.

Along the wall are old cupboards and shelves fixed right up to the ceiling. They are piled high with the stuff her mother finds in the mudflats and on the beach. Anna throws nothing away. Trine carefully shuffles her feet forward without lifting them. Because most of the floor space too is taken up by the sea's treasure and memories, as her mother calls this junk. And it mustn't be broken; even if it is already broken when she find it, it can't be broken further. Only occasionally does Anna take this piece or that and try to do something with it.

But it doesn't happen often, and the attempt is only ever short-lived, and then it doesn't happen again for months, maybe even years. And the most precious and delicate things that Anna finds, such as glass bottles and beautiful shells, she keeps in her bedroom, which looks just like the shed, stuffed from floor to ceiling with odds and ends that the sea has thrown back to its shores.

In the far corner in the back there is a cupboard where her mother keeps a canister of petrol. The girl kneels down, opens the cupboard door and, just as she is about to stretch out her arm to feel for the canister, pulls back with a shudder of horror, so sudden, so concrete, so real, as if someone put a cold hand onto her shoulder. She stops moving. There is only a *clack* as her teeth hit against each other. Then silence. Total silence. And total darkness, because her mother always draws the curtains in front of the two windows in the evening, as if she's scared a ghost might look into her shed and discover what she's been up to. Now Trine wishes that she had left the door slightly ajar for the last remains of the dusk light to seep in.

'Mum?' she whispers. Her voice is shaking.

No reply.

The horror must have come from inside the cupboard. Trine is not scared of mice and spiders. There must be something else inside that has given her the creeps.

She has no choice. She owes it to Carl. The pirate funeral pyre. It's her fault that he is dead, so it's her job to give him a good send-off.

She clenches her mouth and eyes tight shut as if she is about to duck her head underwater. Then she pushes her arm forward and her hand disappears into the pitch-black crevasse.

She feels the top of the canister. Fingers closing around it, and without thinking, she pulls it from the back of the cupboard, knocking over other things that stand in front of it. The racket is short-lived but loud. Trine jumps up and hits her leg against the table. She charges towards the door. Stops. Her mother must have heard the noise. Surely. She will be coming to check. Trine can't rush straight into Anna's arms with the canister in her hands. There is only one solution. The girl has to squeeze into the cupboard. Monsters aren't real, Trine tells herself as she closes the cupboard door from the inside. If only Carl was still alive and with her.

Then she goes numb.

Afterwards, after her mother had found the beautiful pottery piece last summer and had sat with it at the bottom of the dyke for days and then had begun her clay work, afterwards Trine saw her mother once again roaming the mudflats. And she observed her striding back across the salt marshes and through the bogs. And water from the ditches sloshed over the brim of her boots. But Anna didn't care. She strode on. And every now and again, when she didn't notice quickly enough that one or the other boot had got stuck in the mud and she should have stopped in her stride in order to turn and pull it out with both hands, she fell, right onto her front, into the dark-brown, nearly black sludge. And she was soaked to the bone and smeared with dark wet earth. And dark wet earth was stuck in her hair, dangling into her face when she arrived at the cottage, looking like a witch without eyes.

Her mother doesn't seem to have heard the racket. After a while Trine creeps out of the cupboard. As she stands up, she notices that her shorts are wet. But she has no time to think about that. There are worse things in life than peeing yourself, aren't there? Aren't there, Carl?

'Did you hear me?' she whispers, as she once again feels her way around the table and towards the door. Then she clasps the canister to her chest and runs.

Only when Trine gets to the shipwreck does she realize that she's forgotten the matches. Tears are rising. It's all too much. If she could just collapse and dissolve into thin air, like Carl will do soon. But she can't. She can't. She's got this far. She has to finish the task. She climbs up and places the canister next to the duvet. She wants to climb down again to fetch matches when she remembers: Carl always keeps a box of them in his 'treasure jar', hidden under the old fishing nets. This of course isn't a pirate ship. Never was. Trine knows that very well. It used to be a simple fishing boat, her father said. Had lost its way and knew nothing of the perils of the Wattenmeer, off the German west coast. Below deck they would prepare the fish once they had caught them. Slit their throats. Butcher them. Trine and Carl have never eaten fish. And Carl has never ever been below deck. He was scared that the souls of the butchered fish were trapped down there. 'And anyway,' he said, 'a pirate needs the open sea and the open sky. Klaus Störtebeker never slept below deck. Never in his whole life.' Whenever Carl made such sweeping statements, Trine had learned not to second-guess, to take him at his word. Because if not, he would get very angry, accusing her of being far too young to know anything. After all, he had been born long before her.

Trine wishes someone was here to help her. One of her new

friends, Birgit or Katja. It's taken her, Trine, so long to make friends with them. They didn't like her for years. But now they like her. But then again – they would be no good out here.

'A jar is better than a cardboard box,' Carl told his sister. 'A jar with the lid tightly screwed on is water-resistant. A box will only disintegrate in the damp out here.'

He was so clever, so practical. What is she going to do without him!

No thinking. She can't allow herself to think. And she has to hurry. The water is just a couple of metres away now.

She unscrews the canister. She throws the match. The flames flare up and the heat hits her face. She ducks, scurries backwards blindly, nearly falling over the rail. She climbs down, her heart racing, the fire hissing furiously above. When she touches the ground, her legs give way and she falls onto her bum. She is staring intently, doesn't even blink, waiting to see if she can observe something of Carl's body ascending. And maybe his soul too? Trine isn't sure she believes in souls, finds them hard to picture. Pirates didn't believe in souls either, Casper told her. At least not in human souls. Instead, they believed in the souls of the seas and the winds and the fish and the birds. The flames are now dancing high into the dark-purple evening sky. The wood crackles and cracks and snaps. Angry and furious. It won't be long and it will come after her, Trine.

The girl gets to her feet and runs towards the shore.

From now on it will be only Trine and her mother. Carl has gone.

'DID YOU CUT his throat?' Katja leans into Birgit, giggling. They are both sitting on the mattress beneath Elvis Presley.

Birgit and Katja had promised they would come round. And Trine had thought of how to make her room look cool. She dismantled Carl's bedframe; she kept the mattress, though. She'd seen it in one of the magazines in the library. It's a new trend from New York, where in cellar bars they sit on mattresses instead of chairs. She hoped Birgit and Katja would be impressed, not expecting Trine to be up to date with the latest trends. That's also why she pinned a big Elvis Presley poster on the wall above the mattress. Trine doesn't like Elvis, but her friends do because he's American. And they like everything American.

'Wow, we adore Elvis,' Birgit and Katja exclaimed as if from one mouth as they walked in.

Anna also lent Trine the tea set that Otto had bought her when he decided that it was best for her and Carl to stay here in the cottage during the war rather than continue living with him in Berlin. A delicate white china pot with pink flowers and with a handle made of bamboo. And three matching cups.

Trine now pours tea for the three of them and hands her friends each a cup.

'No, I didn't cut his throat,' she replies matter-of-factly to Katja's question.

She knew they would ask about the details but she is no longer sure she wants to share them. Talking about it out loud makes it sounds so banal, so trivial. Though it wasn't trivial at all. But she knows she has to tell them. To become their true friend. That was the deal.

'He fell from the shipwreck and broke his neck.' It was out. She had said it too quickly, without thinking. And now she can't take it back.

'Fell from the shipwreck?' Birgit muses into her cup while she sips her tea.

'If he hadn't fallen, I would have pushed him. I swear.'

Oh God, why did she say that? She comes across so desperate. After all, it's none of their business, her brother. It was her brother, Trine's brother. He belonged to her and to her alone. Why did she ever agree to do this for them?

Because she wants to be their friend. She no longer wants to be stuck with Carl.

They started to tease her about him at school. Last spring. Hauke Müller had somehow found out. In the schoolyard he put his leg out and tripped Trine over. Then the three of them – Hauke, Jens and Norbert – formed a circle around her.

'This brother of yours, we'd like to talk to him.'

Trine had sat up, her knees stinging badly. It took her a moment to process what Hauke had said. She raised herself up. She had never mentioned Carl to anyone. How did they know? She tried to squeeze past them, but Jens stepped in front of her.

'Why aren't you replying, weirdo?'

'What's up, guys?' Birgit and Katja. Arm in arm.

Hauke had been going out with Birgit since Christmas. And Jens was in love with Katja. But Katja played hard to get. All the boys in their year and the year above were in love with either Katja or Birgit. Or both. Many boys weren't choosy.

'The weirdo thinks she's got a brother. But we've never seen him. So we'd like to be introduced to him,' Hauke explained.

'So what?' Katja popped her chewing-gum bubble. 'I've never met your big brother either, have I?'

'No. But you know I have a brother. And everyone knows that I have a brother. How come, then, that we've never heard about the weirdo's brother before?'

Trine was now standing still, stock still, looking down at her feet and the dirty white socks in the dirty brown shoes.

Birgit let go of Katja's arm and gave Hauke a shove to move out of the way.

'Let her be. We'll have a chat with her.'

She put her arm around Trine's shoulder. Katja appeared at Trine's other side. Birgit started walking and pushed Trine gently forward. Trine would have loved to just run away, fearing the worst. More interrogations about her brother. It had nothing to do with any of them. They should just leave her alone. But neither Katja nor Birgit said anything. Silently they walked to the edge of the schoolyard. Then the bell rang for the next lesson.

'Don't worry, they won't bother you again.' Birgit lifted her arm from Trine's shoulders. 'You are now our friend.'

Birgit and Katja had never before talked to Trine. Which was no surprise. They had everything Trine didn't have: breasts and long hair and their periods, and they were even allowed to wear shoes with heels. They understood the boys' jokes and laughed about them. They were fast runners and stars at gymnastics. And they lived in town, where everyone lived except Trine. The only thing that Trine was better at than them was school. But of course that didn't really count. At least not for making friends.

Lots of girls wanted to be Birgit's and Katja's friends. But usually Birgit and Katja just hung out with the boys. Trine didn't believe that she was now their friend. And somehow she didn't believe either that the boys wouldn't pester her again about Carl. But they didn't. And the next day Birgit and Katja came up to Trine during break time and gave her their autograph books to write something inside. Trine couldn't sleep all night. She was trying to figure out what to write or draw or what poem to copy.

Needless to say, Carl was no help in the matter.

'And then, what did you do after he broke his neck? There must have been a body. How did you get rid of the body?' Birgit now enquires.

It had been Trine's idea to kill Carl. Eventually Birgit and Katja wanted to know about Trine's brother. A week before the summer holidays. By then the girls had spent most of the big breaks together. And the rumour had spread fast through their year that Trine was now best friends with Birgit and Katja. They confided in Trine who they had already kissed and who was a good kisser and whose kisses were disgustingly wet. Then one day, when they were sitting under the apple tree in the far corner of the schoolyard, the most prestigious place in the entire school, especially now in the summer, where before – before she became best friends with Birgit and Katja – Trine wouldn't have dreamed of sitting, ever, Katja suddenly said, 'So, this brother of yours, does he exist?'

No one had mentioned Trine's brother again and somehow Trine had hoped that at least Birgit and Katja had forgotten about him. Although of course deep down she knew they wouldn't have. Well, perhaps not forgotten, but at least they might have shrugged off the idea of the brother as one of Hauke's stupid teasers – after all, he had a reputation for saying all sorts of stupid, unbelievable things, like that he had a willy as huge as a goalpost and stuff like that.

Even at home Trine had been slightly more distant to Carl. Didn't play with him immediately after finishing homework and she locked him out of the bathroom when she tried on Mum's lipstick. Carl would have only mocked her if he had seen what she was up to.

Trine now stopped chewing the gum that Katja had given her. She noticed that her jaw was hurting, her skull was hurting. She actually didn't like chewing gum, but it was one of the things she felt she had to get used to if she wanted to have proper friends and not just her brother.

'So, this brother of yours, does he exist?'

It was such a difficult question. How was she supposed to answer? Of course he existed – for her, Trine, that is. She's not stupid or mad. She knows that away from the cottage and the dyke and mudflats and the shipwreck, he isn't real, real as in going to school and playing football with others. Or let's put it this way: when he plays football – because sometimes he goes and leaves Trine alone with just her mother – the others don't see him. But if all that Carl was was a figment of Trine's imagination, living inside her head and nowhere else, why was it so difficult to get rid of him?

She had tried. Yes, Trine had tried. She had told him,

'You are only a ghost, go away!' She had not spoken to him for a couple of days, ignoring him, trying to walk through him. And she had forbidden him from coming to the shipwreck with her. He tolerated her behaviour. When she didn't speak to him and didn't want him to come to the shipwreck, he eventually decided to go off on his bike. And he stayed away for hours. Trine got so worried. Maybe he had gone out into the mudflats. Even on his bike. He was mad enough to do that.

Finally Carl came home. Late that evening. Trine's mother had become so angry with Trine's fussing over Carl's disappearance that the girl had been sent to bed early. Carl crept into the room and quietly undressed. Trine lay very still, pretending to be asleep. But she knew that Carl knew that she was awake. Only when he eventually had snuggled up under his duvet and she could hear his breathing turn deep and regular did she too fall asleep.

So, was Carl real? Did he exist?

Birgit and Katja had told Trine that they never lied to each other. That they always told the truth to each other, even if the truth sounded really silly. Like when Birgit had a crush on Olli, who no one would ever have a crush on – he's got red hair and smells funny and Mechthild, Katja's older sister, said that when he's big he will have red pubes too – yuck! But still once there were two days when Birgit had a crush on Olli after she dreamed about him and he kissed her in the dream and his dream-kissing had been so good. She had told Katja all about it, even though she had worried that Katja would never speak to her again. Because no one really spoke to Olli either.

Which is true. Trine too had never spoken to Olli.

When Birgit told Katja about Olli, Katja didn't laugh. Katja understood. She sometimes had funny crushes too, she admitted. And so, since the Olli crush, they had become even better friends. Really understanding each other.

Trine wanted to be Birgit's and Katja's friend. A true friend. A real friend.

'Yes, he exists—'

The moment it was out she knew she had made a mistake. It sounded wrong. She wanted to continue to explain what she meant by 'exist' - surely Birgit and Katja would understand. After all, Birgit had had a crush on Olli - on Olli, of all people, who bites his nails and eats his bogies - because of a dream.

'Prove it!' They interrupted Trine straight away. As if they had been waiting for that very answer. They exchanged a quick glance but otherwise kept straight faces.

Trine closed her mouth. All of a sudden their friendship appeared on a knife-edge. And if Trine made the wrong move, she was gone. Gone for ever. And her life would be hell from then on.

How could she keep Birgit's and Katja's friendship?

She had to offer them a sacrifice.

'I will kill him,' she said very quietly and very calmly.

And now she says, 'I burned him in the old shipwreck out on the mudflats.'

She is sitting on the floor cross-legged in front of them. Suddenly her jaw pushes forward, in defiance. They think she couldn't do it, kill Carl, because he was in her head. She knows they want evidence. They won't accept mere words. There is the evidence out on the mudflats.

For a moment both Birgit and Katja are silent. Birgit looks into her teacup while Katja stares at a spot somewhere to the side of Trine.

'So that was the reason for the fire,' Katja eventually mumbles. 'We heard about it.'

'Yes.' Trine's voice is firm, almost as if it isn't her own. It comes from deep inside her. She feels that she has for the first time ever surprised her friends – stunned them into silence.

Katja now lifts her eyes. 'How?'

'How what?'

Trine is irritated by that question. Are they still doubting her?

'I poured petrol over the duvet in which he was rolled up. And then set it alight.'

It sounds so professional. She is proud of herself.

Suddenly Birgit leans forward and puts down her half-drunk cup.

'That's arson, you know that, don't you?' She gets up. 'Come on, Katja, we need to go.'

Trine is confused.

'But I thought we were going to spend the afternoon together.'

Her voice suddenly sounds far less firm. Katja has stood up too.

'Yeah, sorry. My mum wants me back home early today. I forgot to tell you.'

And before Trine has time to get up from the floor the two girls are already by the door.

'Bye, then.'

They storm down the stairs. And the front door closes behind them with a big bang.

Trine is now standing in the middle of her room. What has she done wrong? She doesn't get it.

'Carl?' she asks quietly. Maybe he is here, has come back. She could talk to him. He would understand. And make her feel less lonely.

'Carl?'

No reply. Carl has gone.

THE NEXT DAY at school the atmosphere has changed. Trine feels it the moment she walks into the classroom. For a split second everyone appears to have fallen silent, frozen mid-movement, with their heads turned towards the door, towards her, Trine. Within that moment something very odd happens to her. The floor beneath her feet disappears. And then the walls, the classroom, the school building, the playground, the trees - everything disappears, as if it has all evaporated into thin air. But she isn't falling yet. At first she is hovering in a nothingness, a vacuum. Then she begins to slip. Down a crevasse. If she stretched out her arms just a bit she could touch its walls. But they look rugged, solid rock, the palms of her hands would be terribly grazed. So she keeps them tight by her side.

As Trine is falling the thought crosses her mind that she should be scared. After all, everything - her entire world - has already perished, probably down this hole, so why not her too? It's a thought that passes through her mind, but somehow it doesn't feel real enough for her to hold on to. She won't dissolve. This - the entire spectacle of everything disappearing down the crevasse - is meant for her. It is being done for her benefit. She will come out of it OK.

Trine pushes her jaw slightly forward.

And she's back, back in the classroom, standing by the door. The noise continues, the chatting, the eating, the copying of homework. But as she walks towards her place at the back, the surreptitious looks of Katja, Birgit, Hauke, Jens and Norbert follow her.

Doris is sitting in her place. No one ever sits in her place. It isn't a place anyone fights over. Once you sit at the back of the class you are stigmatized as an outcast. Burned into your flesh, a brand that is impossible to remove.

'This is my place,' Trine says, because she doesn't know what else to say.

'Trine! Here!'

Trine looks over her shoulder. Birgit is pointing to an empty seat between her and Katja in the second row, just behind Hauke. Katja, who normally sits next to Birgit, has moved into Doris's former place.

Trine turns back to Doris, who holds her hands folded in her lap, her shoulders and head hanging forward. Is she crying?

'I'm sorry,' Trine mumbles.

But as she walks towards the front to take her new seat, it strikes her that this was the wrong thing to say. She instinctively senses that the new position allocated to her has to do with the fire she started on the shipwreck. An act of bravery, courageous and violent. From the outside. From the viewpoint of the others. She hasn't thought about it in those terms before. But Trine is clever enough to know that what has impressed everyone else is that she dared to do something that none of the Birgits and Haukes of this world would ever risk. They talk the talk, but they don't walk the walk.

Carl told her that a long time ago, when Trine was crying because of them.

'Whatever they say goes. Goes in the entire school. They don't like me and therefore no one in class likes me or even dares talk to me.'

Carl, good old Carl. Oh, how much she misses him. He simply shrugged his shoulders in his Carl-ish way.

'I like you. And they are just made of air. Lots of breath to talk and no muscles to fight.'

Trine remembers him sitting opposite her, across the little campfire that they sometimes made with sticks and some newspaper in the tin that they kept hidden inside the shipwreck. They were smoking a cigarette that Trine had secretly taken from her mother and Carl was holding it very coolly between the tips of his thumb and middle finger. He could already smoke without coughing. Trine was still struggling.

'Your time will come,' Carl continued, exhaling and vanishing behind a smoky screen. 'And then they will bow to you in awe and adoration.'

'Carl, can you see me now?' Trine's lips don't move, but she forms this question clearly inside her head, hoping that her brother will hear her. Wherever he may be.

THEY WANT TO look at what is left of the old shipwreck. Trine hasn't been back into the mudflats – hasn't even ventured beyond the dyke – since she started the fire. But she knows there is still something there. Her mother has said so. And the big autumn storms that might carry off what is now left of the ship haven't yet started. But it won't be long. The sea lavender has died down and the brent geese have returned.

Trine would have preferred not to go back. But she doesn't want to disappoint her friends.

At the bottom of the dyke they take off their shoes and socks. The blue sky is cloudless. A flock of oystercatchers is heading out towards the sea, which is nothing more than a thin line on the horizon.

Already as they walk through the salt marshes, Birgit and Katja begin to complain. The grass is cutting their feet. Their moaning intensifies as Trine leads them straight through the deepest oozing mud where the dark-blue sludge smells of eggy farts.

'Who farted? Yuck. Who farted?' Hauke doubles over.

Birgit wretches, while the boys love it. That was Trine's intention. She is sure that she's the only one among them who knows the mudflats well. The others might not live far from the coast, the town is only three kilometres away, but at best they have done the odd Sunday afternoon walk with their parents around here at low tide, or at high tide come for a swim during the summer holidays.

'I'm not going further,' Katja suddenly says in a voice close to tears. 'Mudflats can be dangerous, you know. We can sink in too deep and never get out again.'

'Uhuu, little Katja is scared.'

Whose voice was that? Trine freezes. It was inside her head, that's for sure. Carl? It could have been. And now, for the first time since they came over the top of the dyke, she directs her gaze towards the shipwreck. And there it is, looking surprisingly untouched by the fire. Trine imagined it coal black, with a hull charred to thin paper waiting for the next gust of wind to blow it away. But no. From this angle one can't even tell that there was a fire. It must have blown out quickly. But didn't she see and feel the flames rising high into the sky? What if they suddenly don't believe her any longer - don't believe that she set Carl ablaze?

'You stay where you are, Katja.'

Her tone is sharp. She has no time for sissy behaviour. She continues walking towards the wreck without looking back. She has to get there first. Check it out first.

She climbs the rope ladder, jumps over the railing - and nearly falls right down into what used to be below deck but is now nothing more than a burnt-out shell. For a moment she struggles to keep her balance until her hands manage to regrip the barrier behind her. She throws a quick glance down. Charred wood and ash. Nothing else. Not even a shred of the quilt. Tears shoot into her eyes. Oh, how she hopes that there is nothing left of Carl in this terrible emptiness.

She feels movement behind. Hauke is about to climb the ladder.

'Wait till I come down.'

When he looks over the railing, his assessment is not too dissimilar from Trine's.

'Wow, nothing there.'

But she doesn't like the tone of his voice. He has no right

to make such statements. As if he's judging her. No, worse, as if he's judging Carl. That's what Hauke's tone sounds like to her. Why did she bring them here? The shipwreck, the mudflats, Carl – they belong to her. To her alone. Her new friends have nothing to do with this. She feels anger rising. They are intruders, invaders – and she brought them here. But the anger is not directed towards herself. It's directed towards them.

As they came up to the shipwreck, she had noticed a paddle. And if she isn't mistaken, she even saw a jellyfish in it. She now strolls over to it, bends down and picks it up – a beautiful yellow compass jellyfish with tentacles that are almost as long as Trine's arm. It can't do any harm to humans. But she'd be surprised if the others knew that.

'Who's ready for a jellyfish fight!' She waves the fish in front of Norbert, who's standing closest to her.

Birgit and Katja shriek, hugging each other and hiding their faces inside their arms. For a few seconds Norbert appears frozen to the spot.

'I'll fight your jellyfish.'

Hauke has now descended from the wreck and steps forward, pushing Norbert aside.

'You'll have to find your own, then.'

Hauke lets his searching glance travel across the dark, oozing, sizzling ground.

'There aren't any.'

Trine was waiting for him to say that. Summer is over, so the jellyfish have gone again. Hers is a lone survivor. Truth to tell, she would never have suggested a jellyfish fight if it had been for real. She doesn't like jellyfish fights. Carl didn't like them either. It's cruel to the jellyfish. She kneels down and gently puts the creature back into its puddle. Then, before any of the others have had time to notice what she's about to do, she scoops up a handful of mud and throws it straight into Hauke's face. Hard and unerringly.

'Then how about a mud fight?'

She doesn't wait for a reply, but has already picked up the next handful and thrown it straight at Norbert. The girls scream and run off to the side. But the boys don't need much of an invitation. And soon they are throwing mud at each other and Trine, rubbing it into their faces and all over their clothes and their hair, then throwing themselves right down into it and rolling around, laughing hysterically.

'You look terrible!' Birgit and Katja are staring at the four of them lying in the mud, exhausted and breathless.

'And you are wicked, Trine.' Hauke's head is very close to hers and briefly their temples touch.

IN THE EVENING, Trine can't fall asleep. She has butterflies in her tummy and everywhere under her skin. When her new friends had gone, she wanted to talk to Carl. Really badly. But then she realized that he would probably be the worst person to talk to. He's far too young to understand what she is now feeling - especially for Hauke. Oddly, she never thought anything much about Hauke before. She and Carl always agreed that Hauke was a bully. But suddenly her opinion of him appears to have changed. Because he admires her now. And he thinks her far more wicked and daring than Birgit and Katja. That is clear. And when his temple touched hers, that was no coincidence. Oh no! Not with Hauke.

Trine gets out of bed and scurries to the bathroom. She closes the door quietly, turns on the little light above the mirrored cupboard and opens it, then takes out her mother's make-up bag. She just wants to see what she looks like with a bit of mascara on. And maybe some blue eyeshadow and some lipstick.

Trine likes what she sees in the mirror. It makes her look older. She lifts her nightie and examines her chest. Nothing there yet. She makes a fist and hits her nipples, then pinches them hard between her fingertips. No pain either. Will she ever grow any breasts? She needs to get a bra from somewhere. Some girls who haven't got much yet either still wear bras and stuff them with cotton wool. Trine has observed them at sports lessons.

The next day after school she doesn't bicycle straight home. Instead she heads to the department store in town. She hasn't got any money. She only wants to try on some bras, see what it feels like for when she does have breasts. Birgit already has proper breasts. And they are real. So Hauke clearly likes girls with breasts.

In the store she looks for a shop assistant. Birgit wears pink lace bras. But Trine worries that the lace will itch. To her dad's funeral her mother made her wear a black lace blouse. It was horrible, she couldn't stop itching while the pastor spoke at the church. Trine walks through the aisles, looking for help. But no one is around. All day she had sat in class imagining what she'd look like in a bra. And how, if she found a really nice bra, one that might almost fit her, maybe she would be able to persuade her mother to come with her next Saturday so that she could see for herself and perhaps even buy it. Once again, Trine feels her jaw pushing forward. It doesn't suit the new Trine - the Trine after Carl - to give up. Does it? She focuses harder on the bras on display. Eventually she reaches a small section at the back that says in big pink letters: Your First Bra. That's what she's been looking for. Is she allowed to open the boxes, take the bras out, try them on? No one around. She opens a box. The material is soft between her fingers. She picks a light-blue, a dark-blue and a pink one in their boxes and walks towards the changing rooms. Again, no one there either. In a cubicle she drops her satchel and coat to the floor, pulls off her jumper and vest. Pulls the dark-blue bra over her head. She slips out of her shoes and pulls off her socks and slips them inside the cups. She puts her vest back on to see if one could tell the difference. As real as with the other girls who stuff their bras, Trine concludes. And even Birgit adds some cotton wool. Things aren't always how they appear with Birgit. Oh no. A lot of breath to talk and not so much muscle for action. She, Trine, is different. She's about to take off her vest again - after all, she now knows what she will show her mother - when her eyes fall on the price tag. That's a lot of money. Her mother won't buy it for her. She peeps around the curtain of her cubicle. Still no one. She acts quickly. Finishes dressing. Closes the boxes. Makes sure she is holding the empty box between the other two as she returns them to their place. She isn't looking up, so she doesn't know if there are any shop assistants around now. She walks calmly out of the shop and down the road. She jumps on her bike and cycles faster than ever before, bent deep over the handlebars. Back home, in her room, she throws herself onto the bed and buries her giggling, hot face in the pillow.

IT ISN'T THAT Trine is in love with Hauke. She definitely isn't. But she loves the way he admires her now. For some reason, she feels his admiration is more real than that of Birgit and Katja, who only became friendly with her because they smelt a good story with Carl. They wanted evidence that Trine was playing embarrassingly childish games with her brother and that that brother didn't even exist. Then they would have gone to Hauke and told him all about it, in the hope that Trine would have become the laughing stock of the entire school and that Hauke and his mates would have been impressed by Birgit and Katja getting out of Trine what they themselves had failed to extract from her. So, Birgit and Katja's admiration for Trine had only ever been something to do with the boys. While Hauke's admiration is about no one other than her.

And of course Birgit doesn't like it at all.

'I let him touch my fanny,' Birgit says, and takes a puff from her cigarette.

Trine continues rolling her cigarette, pretending she didn't hear or it didn't matter to her.

'Really?' Katja shrieks with excitement, next to Trine. 'So what was it like? Did you touch his thing too?'

'You mean his dick?' Birgit says, and takes another drag.

Katja nods. 'Was it hard?'

Birgit stares into the distance, a smile playing around the corners of her mouth. It's a show, Trine senses, played out for her benefit. But she pretends not to notice, not to care.

'Next time we'll do it. He's already put his finger inside me,' Birgit then adds.

'Oh wow!'

Katja has forgotten that she is holding a cigarette and ash drops onto the mattress. They are sitting in Trine's room. It's a good hang-out. Trine's mother spends most afternoons walking along the beaches, or in her shed, while Birgit's and Katja's mothers are always at home. Here they can even smoke.

Birgit ignores Katja's comment.

'In fact we – Hauke and I – were wondering if we could borrow your room, Trine.' She makes a vague circling movement with her head, pointing to all four corners of Trine's room. 'Tomorrow after school.' She pauses. 'If, of course, your mum is out.'

Trine has finished rolling her cigarette. She slowly lifts it up to her lips and lets her tongue travel along the paper. Then she presses the paper down with her index fingers. Slowly.

'Tomorrow's no good,' she lies.

She puts the cigarette between her lips and holds out a hand for Birgit to pass her the lighter. She lights the cigarette. Inhales.

'But Monday is possible.'

That gives her the entire weekend.

Trine is disappointed that Hauke doesn't see through Birgit. Doesn't he realize that the fact she allows him to touch her has nothing to do with him? That it is all to do with the competition between Birgit and Trine. Birgit doesn't want to lose him to Trine. That's all. If there were no Trine, Birgit would not allow him to touch her fanny or put his finger inside her or anything. But then again, does it matter to Hauke what

Birgit's motivation are, as long as he gets what he wants? And maybe he wants that. Maybe he wants sex.

Over the last couple of weeks, Trine's breasts have finally started to grow. Not by much, mind, but a bit. And Trine knows all about sex. Ever since the summer, since she no longer shares a room with Carl, she has discovered the pleasures of touching herself. One time she woke up because her heart was racing and her body tingling and her hand underneath her nightie. When she realized it wasn't a dream, she froze and held her hands tight above her tummy. But then she wanted to know if she had caused that beautiful feeling inside herself. It was pitch dark and there was no sound, not from outside or inside the house. She moved a hand onto her crotch. There it lay for a while as she listened to her own breathing. Then she remembered what she had done in the dream and briefly she felt nothing. But slowly, very slowly, the butterflies entered her tummy. And then eventually something like a wave took hold of her body and her mind and for a moment she felt incredibly happy because her body and her mind were gone, lifted up and away on the crest of the wave. And even when she was put back down again onto the bed, into the dark, she felt as if anything was possible. As if there were no limits. She loved the feeling. Of course she knew that real sex, the sort everyone was talking about and sniggering about and wanting to do, had to do with putting someone's penis into your vagina. So she saved a big piece of cucumber from her lunch box and the following night put it inside her. Initially carefully, then a bit further. It was slightly uncomfortable. Strange. Really quite funny thinking she had a cucumber in her fanny. But that was it. It didn't even hurt. And there was no blood. Wasn't there supposed to be blood if you do it for the first time? She'd read that in a book from the library. Maybe she wasn't normal. Maybe everyone lied. Maybe it was only good for the boys.

Trine would like to ask Birgit: Do you really want to do it? Trine of course doesn't know if Birgit is touching herself, but she doubts it. Or Katja. It feels so illicit, so forbidden. And Katja and Birgit are such pretty-pretty girls. Smoking is the most wicked thing they do.

Up to now.

Now Birgit is willing to go all the way. To outdo Trine.

But Trine will not be outdone by Birgit.

'YOU AND BIRGIT want to borrow my room?'

Hauke is standing in Trine's room. She has brought him here on the pretext that she can help him prepare for the maths test the next day. But that's not really the reason. He followed her, didn't even ask for clarification, even though Trine knows that he isn't that interested in maths. Still, she sees it as a good omen. Maybe he too has just been waiting for an excuse to be alone with her.

'Yeah,' he now says. 'If that's all right with you.'

She shrugs her shoulders. 'Sure. Wait here. I'll be right back.'

Trine heads into the bathroom. For a minute or so she just sits on the edge of the bathtub. He's never even attempted to kiss her. And besides that one time when their temples touched, in the mudflats, he's never touched her again. Trine's no fool. Even if she's never had a boy fancy her, she's aware that Hauke is not in love with her. Nor is he, however, in love with Birgit. Trine might perhaps have liked to be in love with Hauke. But she stopped that feeling as soon as she became aware of it. It would have weakened her and he would have smelt her weakness. If there is one thing you have to be careful about with someone like Hauke it's not to show weakness. Trine has to be in a position of strength. Of control. Then she will have Hauke's respect. She learned this lesson from Klaus Störtebeker, who, even after he was beheaded, managed to pick himself up and walk past eleven of his crew members in an attempt to save them. To be strong and courageous at all times. Even if the odds are stacked against you.

Trine takes off her clothes. Then she kneels down and lifts the loose corner of the linoleum underneath the sink. Yesterday after school she headed to the chemist's department in the big store. She's become good in pocketing the odd, necessary items she requires. She never overdoes it, though. Never steals more than one or two things a month. She only took a small packet. She's not intending to repeat this experiment. It's a service she's offering to Hauke. So he won't embarrass - or maybe even humiliate himself - in front of Birgit.

Trine removes the condom she has hidden underneath the linoleum and makes sure that the corner is pressed down well again.

'What the—'

Hauke was sitting on the mattress but now he jumps up, backing away a couple of steps towards the wall.

'I thought you should practise.' Trine rehearsed the sentence, over and over again, yesterday evening and then got up early to practise it again this morning. Deep, steady voice. 'For when you do it with Birgit.'

She's standing in the doorframe. Hasn't moved. He too now stands as if nailed to the floor, concentrating on her face, avoiding looking at her naked body, she notices.

'I don't need any practice.'

His voice is hoarse. He swallows hard. He's never thought of Trine in this way, like she has the body of a woman. And she doesn't. He can see it from the corner of his eyes. There are no proper breasts for a start.

'Really?' She raises an eyebrow like in the movies.

She has to stay in control. She can't back down now. She

thinks again of Klaus Störtebeker, who carried his head underneath his arm as he walked past the eleven men standing next to each other. Eleven men! How many metres is that? Ten at least. She has to cross less than ten metres to reach Hauke. Much less.

'So you've done it before?'

There is a cold draught from the corridor stroking her back. Goosebumps are spreading across her body.

'Yes.'

Hauke shakes his head and looks like a little boy to Trine. She comes a step closer.

'Then you can show me.' She closes her eyes to a slit.

'I . . . I . . .' He takes another step back, hits with his heel against the leg of the bed.

She needs to make the next move quickly, before he recovers the power of speech. Before he decides to just leave the room. She angles her foot back and kicks the door shut. She takes another step towards Hauke. The condom. She's forgotten she's holding the condom. She lifts her hand and tucks it behind her ear. She's next to him now.

'We don't have to kiss,' she says.

She's aware that he could just push her aside, storm out. She unzips his jeans. Because she is looking down, avoiding his face, she notices that he's stopped breathing. She kneels and opens the laces of his shoes, then takes first one heel, then the other and eases his feet out. He's not resisting. She pulls down his jeans and his pants. And once again she lifts his feet, one by one, to pull them away. She stands up. Her gaze briefly brushes across his crotch. Nothing is happening. It's hanging.

'Let's lie down,' she says, and takes him by his wrist.

She wants to pull him towards the mattress, but he frees himself with one swift movement, resisting her.

'Trine, listen. I like you . . .' He hesitates. 'But not in that way.'

He bends down to pick up his clothes. He tries not to look at her, although there is nothing more he wants to do at the moment – keeping her in his sight. She scares him. She always scared him a bit. But he liked that, being scared a bit, as long as it was only a bit. Now it is no longer a bit. She scares him. Seriously. What normal girl would undress herself and then undress him!

He gathers up his pants and jeans. Luckily he can just put his foot through both without separating them. As he uncurls his spine to pull up one jeans leg high enough to step into the other, he feels a thump against his shoulders. He tumbles back against the wall. Pain shoots up his spine. He falls over – too fast to let go of his jeans in order to free his hands and protect himself from slumping down hard on the floor. He's pinned down on this back and she straddles his belly. He feels her weight, her strength. She's much stronger than she looks.

'If you move or scream or shout, you are dead,' she whispers. And he believes her. Her face hovers over his. He smells her breath.

Something wet crawls down his cheek.

'Are you crying, you baby?' She brings her face even closer. He turns his head to the side, desperately trying not to cringe while her tongue wipes across his right cheek.

'So, shall we play our little game now? Shall I show you how it's done?'

Trine has no idea what has got into her. This hadn't been

planned. She's never envisaged it. It's his fear - she can smell it, her nose travelling now over his ear and down his throat and up his chin and across his mouth. His fear excites her, makes her powerful.

He's wiggling underneath her, kicking his legs up behind her.

'Let me go. I don't like you,' his voice whines.

A whingeing crybaby, that's what he is.

'You are weird,' he whimpers. 'Let me go.'

His body moves underneath her and she feels as if she's on a ship on a rough, stormy sea. This is going too far. He is going too far. He's no longer obeying her. She lets go of his shoulders and in the next moment she brings her interlinked hands down in a mighty fist on his chest. Carl taught her that move. Instantaneously Hauke goes floppy, fighting for his breath.

She bends forward again, licking once more across his cheek. First one side, then the other. Then she stretches out, lying down flat on him.

'I can't breathe,' he wails.

'Psst, my lovely,' she whispers. 'You clearly can breathe. If you can cry and whinge and whimper, you can breathe too.'

She puts her head by the side of his neck, waiting for his breathing to become regular. And also because for a moment she is out of ideas. What if nothing is happening between his legs? What will she do then? Lying on top of him, the only hard edges she feels are his bones sticking out everywhere. She didn't think he'd be so thin.

'I will sit up now,' she whispers. 'If you try to run away, or make a noise, or anything else silly, you are dead.' She pauses. 'Dead like my brother,' she adds.

She sits up and slides back down his legs, then sits on his knees. He still has his head turned to the side, his eyes squeezed tight shut. She shrugs her shoulders. No need for them to look at each other while doing it.

She looks at his floppy willy. It is tiny. Hauke always bragged about his big one. A joke. Birgit is in for a disappointment. Trine smiles.

She pushes her index finger underneath it and flicks it over.

'You need to relax.' She hits him with her flat hand across the chest. But playfully. She shouldn't frighten him any more.

'I can't,' he squeezes out from between his closed lips.

For a moment she stares at his tense face. He's a chicken. A wet chicken. Pathetic. Now she would love to just get up and walk out of the room, get dressed again and then walk back in here to find him gone. And then she would get rid of the mattress and the stupid poster on the wall. Maybe she would put her brother's bed back. But maybe not. Probably not. And when she's older she'd do it with a proper man. Someone she finds handsome, really handsome. Even with his clothes off.

Still, none of this is an option. She has to see through what she's started. If only to keep face. And show Hauke who's pulling the strings here.

'So what do you do when you're on your own to get this—' she nods towards his willy – 'going?'

'What do you mean?'

All of a sudden, her voice sounds soft and warm. That's why he opens his eyes. That's why he turns his head and looks at her. He didn't want to.

'This,' she repeats, nodding towards his willy.

She's strong and he doesn't want to risk being hit again. He really couldn't breathe just now and it wasn't a nice feeling.

And yes, he doesn't fancy her. Doesn't fancy her at all. Her face isn't pretty and her body isn't pretty – not like Birgit's at least – but if the only way he can get out of here is by doing it, so be it. There could be worse things. And then at least he's done it and it will put him miles ahead of the other guys. He won't need to tell them who he's done it with. She won't tell either. That's one thing he's sure about.

He moves his right hand towards his willy. Slowly, so that Trine doesn't think he wants to escape or hit her, he closes his fingers to a fist around it. Her eyes are glued to his hand. He begins to move his fist up and down. Instinctively, he closes his eyes as he always does. But then he opens them again and watches her watching his hand. It's a nice feeling – he can't deny it – how she watches. Her attention.

His willy begins to stir. Thank God.

His movements become faster. He closes his eyes again. Then he rips them open. He was about to forget himself. Now he's hard. Let's see if she stays true to her word. She isn't pretty but she isn't exactly ugly either.

He stops. Opens his fist. She's still staring.

'There,' he says.

He wouldn't mind putting it inside her now. Really wouldn't mind. He loves the way she watches him. Her eyelashes are beautiful, dark and long. He hadn't noticed before.

For a moment she doesn't move. Finally she lifts her glance. Avoiding his eyes, she looks around. Then she leans over towards the left. When she comes to sit straight in front of him again, she's holding the condom packet in her fingers. With her teeth she rips it open and concentrates on getting the condom out. She's practised this too. Yesterday. On a cucumber. Again. She's never liked cucumber but now they have finally come into their own. She notices her heart galloping, aware that she has to touch his thing. That she's never touched a willy before. It looks somehow ugly. Vile. Why do women want to put it inside themselves?

'Here, let me do it,' he says, and takes the condom out of her fingers and unrolls it over his willy.

He too must have practised. She wonders if the boys practise together.

She gives herself a push. She needs to finish the job. Think about Birgit, she hears a voice inside her head saying. You need to get there first. You will get there first.

She lifts her bum from his legs and shuffles forward on her knees until she's right over his erect penis. He's holding it at the bottom. She lowers herself down, concentrating to make sure it doesn't miss the hole. It doesn't. She feels it at the entrance. Then in one go she pushes down, thinking about the cucumber. It was a big cucumber, bigger than this willy of his. She stops. Waits. Pain? No. Her eyes were fixed on his bony chest. Now she lifts them and looks into his face. Their eyes meet. Only for a split second. Then she looks away again. Looking into his eyes somehow disturbed her concentration.

'Move up and down,' she hears him say.

She does.

At first Trine looks at the wall behind him. She concentrates on a dirty mark about thirty centimetres – a ruler's length – above the mattress and maybe half a metre beneath the poster. She doesn't want to look at the poster. She hates Elvis Presley. She hates his big ears, his high forehead, his bendy legs. And she doesn't want to look at Hauke's face. His eyes are squeezed tightly together. His mouth open. Pathetic. The dirty mark comforts her. It's where Carl's bed stood against the wall. Maybe Carl's head touched there. Her glance once again brushes briefly across Hauke's face. Distorted and ugly. That's what it is. She wishes she had a camera and could take a picture. And then hang it up in the classroom. Just for fun. What a laugh. She turns her head to the left, scanning the floor. For no particular reason, except to avoid his face. She's fine with the movement. In fact it's like sitting on a horse. Not that she's ever sat on a real horse. But it doesn't matter. Or better: it didn't matter, when Carl was still around. Pirates didn't ride horses. They only sailed their ships across the oceans. Anyway, that's beside the point – it's all in the past, her and Carl's past. The point is that whatever she's doing here at the moment feels as close to riding a horse as she can imagine. She certainly doesn't feel anything else. No butterflies in her tummy. But she shouldn't be dismissive. No, she shouldn't. She's doing 'it' with Hauke.

'Faster,' she hears Hauke groan. 'Faster.'

She moves faster. Her thighs begin to hurt. But she can't help feeling that this will soon end.

She turns her head to the other side, avoiding Hauke's face. No need to see it again. Revolting.

And then. Just at the moment when Hauke seems to go totally mental beneath her, he stops. And then convulses. Just in that moment she loses her balance and falls forward right onto him, onto his face. Then he lies still. She lies still.

'Ouch. I can't breathe,' she hears Hauke plead from underneath her body.

She rolls off him to the side.

'What did you do that for?'

She shrugs her shoulders. 'I was just exhausted.' It's something to say.

'Really?' A brief beam lights up his face, although he would have liked to hide it.

Jerk! She sits up. From the corner of her eye she notices his limp willy with the end of the condom now filled with white liquid.

Yuck. She suppresses a retch that is travelling up her throat.

'Time to go.'

She rises. Picks up his jeans and holds them out to him.

He hasn't moved. Instead he pushes his arms underneath his head, looking up at her. From this angle she really doesn't look bad. Not bad at all.

'You were good,' he says.

As if he knew. Had plenty of comparisons. But then again, he only knows that he hasn't much to go on. His performance just now didn't betray his inexperience. Far from it. Clearly. It exhausted her to the point of collapse. Poor love.

He smiles up at her.

For a moment his arrogance has thrown her off balance. Then she drops his jeans onto his stomach.

'My mum will be back shortly. You better go. And take everything—' with a nod of her head, she points to his crotch – 'with you.'

She steps over him and walks out of the room and into the bathroom. She sits down on the bathtub and waits for the front door to open and close. But it doesn't. Hauke must still be in her room. She doesn't know what to do. She doesn't want to see him again. At least not today. She needs time to think. What she's just done with Hauke is bad for a girl. And she doesn't really understand why she's done it with him. She just wanted to see what it was like. And yes, she didn't like it that Hauke was touching Brigit's fanny. But did she need to go all the way? He would never have done it with her otherwise, would he? She waits a bit longer. Then she dresses herself, carefully opens the door and on tiptoes sneaks down the stairs. She grabs her jacket on the way but not her shoes. She's heading into the mudflats. She doesn't need them there. She and Carl only ever wore wellies or boots in the winter. And even then they sometimes took them off. Just for fun.

As she's walking down the dyke on the other side, she hears someone running up behind her. Before she has time to turn her head and look over her shoulder, Hauke is next to her.

'Can I come with you?' he pants, out of breath from catching up with her.

'I'm not going anywhere. I just want to watch the clouds.' It comes out more defiant than she had intended. But she doesn't know how to take his appearance.

'I like watching clouds too.'

He notices her naked feet and, hardly slowing down, he slips out of his shoes. He'll pick them up on the way back. His socks are in his pockets anyhow. When he saw Trine leaving the house he didn't waste time putting them on.

They cross the salt marshes in silence. Big cumulus clouds are moving across the vast blue sky, while sharp-edged afternoon sunlight glitters on the mudflats. Hauke's hand briefly brushes past Trine's. She pretends she hasn't noticed. Maybe it was just coincidence. Then she feels his fingers hesitantly interlinking with hers.

ANNA

ANNA PULLS THE man out of the water, kneels down, puts her ear to his mouth. He's breathing. She turns him on his side, begins hitting his back. Then she stops. More importantly, now she has to get him out of the cold. They are both soaking wet and her teeth are chattering. She strokes the hair out of his face. It's him. The man she met the other day.

The fog was thick that morning. A white, silent, stagnant soup. And she was right in the middle of it. She could see neither land nor waterline. Her brain was struggling to process what her senses could take in. Just a moment ago she had mistaken a lone plover running away from her for a grey furry ball being blown across her path by the wind. What wind? There was no wind that morning. Not even the stirrings of a faint breeze. She squeezed her eyes into narrow slits and focused hard. Vertical lines are so rare out here that the eye tends to overlook them until they are right in front of you – even in clear weather.

The man was walking towards her. His grey trousers were halfway up his shins, he was barefoot. As always when she encounters a stranger – which over the past fourteen years has rarely happened because she goes to town only once a month to do errands and otherwise never leaves the sea – she quickly checked in her mind how old Carl would be now. Thirty-two. So could this be him? Sometimes she wishes she didn't feel she had to wait any longer, to ask herself these questions, to check how old Carl would be. But she can't help it. Waiting has become part of her being – her physical and psychological being – like an arm or a leg. She has no idea now how to be without waiting any longer.

She doesn't want to leave the man on his own while she runs to get help. She tells herself it's because he might head back into the water. At the moment, he's unconscious. But he might not be for long. The grey sky smells of snow. The tide is about to turn. He probably thought that if he came out here at low tide on a day like today no one would be here. But she's been roaming the beaches for years. She stands up, bends forward, threads her arms through the man's armpits, crosses them over in front of his chest and begins to pull him towards the marshes, walking backwards. Her wet clothes are slowing her down. She halts, takes off her boots, her anorak, her trousers and her thick jumper. Takes off the man's coat. Only now does she realize he has stones in his pockets. Don't stop to think: He didn't want you to rescue him. Every drowning man wants to be rescued. She shakes her head. She strips him down to his underpants, leaves their clothes in a pile and continues dragging him. The icy air is biting into her skin, whipping it, cutting it. She's moving. He isn't. She leans forward, brings her face close to his.

The man was heading straight for her, approaching fast. When he emerged fully out of the white fog, she slowed her pace. There are fathers, husbands, sons believed long dead who return home after many years. Even now, so many years after the war has ended. But this man was older than Carl would be. She could see his features clearly now. Judging by his deeply furrowed face, with what appeared to be grey stubble on cheeks and chin, he must be in his forties. Difficult to judge. And now he smiled as if they knew each other, revealing his bad teeth, two missing, one at the bottom front and one at the top, the others greyish yellow. It was obvious he was a man who had had a rough life.

He's still breathing. She's slow, too slow, walking backwards like this. She turns the man onto his belly, goes down on her knees, pulls him onto her back, with his arms over her shoulders. Bent forward by his weight, she continues on her way. The physical contact keeps them both warmer. After a while, however, she changes again, pulling him backwards to the edge of the sand. Where the marshes start, she carries him on her back once more, his feet dragging through the grass. Her feet are lumps of ice, she can no longer feel the frozen grass.

They were now only a couple of metres away from each other. The man appeared to have slowed down too.

She could smell him. He smelt as if he hadn't washed for days. She noticed his big calloused hands, the ring finger missing from his right hand, which was holding a sailor's sack slung over his shoulder.

Anna used to fantasize that Carl might have been saved by a big piece of driftwood. Clinging on to it, maybe he was carried across the waters almost to the shores of England, where he could have been picked up by a British trawler. They would have put him in an internment camp, but eventually they'd send him back. Maybe he had lost his memory. But now by chance – perhaps he worked on shrimp boats up and down the coast – he had arrived back here.

The man nodded. '*Guten Morgen.*'

Halfway up the dyke, Anna stumbles and falls flat on her face. The man is now lying on top of her. For a few seconds she feels as if she will never be able to get up again. Hot tears burn her frozen cheeks. It has started to snow. Thick snowflakes.

'*Guten Morgen,*' she replied. Stopped.

The man didn't stop. He walked past her.

And during those fleeting moments when she had stopped and the man had walked past her, a familiar film had once again played in her mind – a film she herself made years ago. Or rather, started making years ago. She'd never got beyond the first scene. But that scene plays out in her mind whenever she encounters a stranger.

Scene I: Anna has invited the man back to the cottage. She's laid the table. The man is picking up the delicate teacup. He can't recall ever having held such delicate china between his fingers. Anna notices the man's hand shaking and regrets not having used the pottery mugs. Not because she's worried he might break one of her good cups. But she doesn't seem to have succeeded in putting him at ease. She decided on the good cups because she wanted to show him that she was making an effort.

She says, 'Tell me about yourself. What has happened to you?'

The man carefully puts the cup back down onto the saucer.

He hasn't yet taken a sip. When the tea touched his lips it was still too hot. It now crosses his mind that the woman isn't asking him to tell her stories from his childhood so that she can check if they are true or false. She's asking him to talk about what has happened to him. For a split second he glances at the cake. He would like to take a forkful, he hasn't eaten anything yet for breakfast. But then he forces himself to focus on the woman's question.

And he tells her everything that he remembers. He leaves nothing out.

A British boat fished him out of the ice-cold North Sea. The first thing he remembers is waking up in an internment camp hospital. Apparently he had mumbled some words in German. He had been adrift on a large wooden pallet. He could speak German, that was true, and he understood a few phrases in English, like 'What's your name?' But he had no idea how to answer such questions. He couldn't remember his name, or where he came from, or what had happened. Nothing. And it stayed that way. At first they thought he might be a spy. They asked him if he wanted to choose a name for himself. He shook his head. They named him Felix Fish. They also gave him a birthdate: 1 January 1927.

In the first few months there were many nights in the camp when the man tried to remember. Anything. Why could he remember the language but not anyone saying anything? He even remembered some tunes, he sang them to the other inmates. They were common nursery rhymes that most mothers would sing to their children. Since his brain didn't yield much, he lay awake at night listening to his body. Bodies remember, don't they? But no images, no sounds, no smells came to mind.

Eventually the Tommies released him and sent him back. And as soon as he arrived in Germany, in Hamburg harbour where he disembarked, everything felt so familiar. He was drunk with familiarity. And he mistook the familiarity for memory. He was sure that he knew the place. That he had been here before. He walked around in a daze. He recognized smells, he recognized voices, he recognized street signs, the way people walked, the way they held themselves, the way they talked, the way they laughed. In the first week again and again he would stop a woman, a man, even some children in the street, saying, '*Mutti? Vati?* Do you recognize me? It's me!' But again and again people looked at him blankly, often pushing him aside. Only occasionally someone would say, apologetically, as if they would have liked to help him by knowing him, '*Nein, tut mir leid.*'

That first week back in Germany broke his heart. He hadn't been prepared for the hope that gripped him the moment he stepped off the boat. Hope that had made itself small - very small - while he was far away, where like any strong young man he had felt he didn't really need a family. He didn't even need memory. That's what he thought while he was abroad. And who knew what was in his past? It might be better not to know anyway, now that the war was over.

But the past is a strange beast. You need a past to push forward into the future. If you don't have a past you don't have any mass or weight to anchor you, to lend you velocity. Then you are nothing more than a ghost.

The only thing that was able to provide comfort was alcohol. It was cheap and plentifully available, and it offered release and friendship too. Lots of different friendships. And the young man understood he wasn't alone, he wasn't the only one without a past. He was surrounded by similar people. Most of them because they wanted to forget. But it came to the same thing. The past was past. It might as well not have happened. Germany was full of people without a past who had woken up without memory in May 1945. And the man finally felt at home.

He began working on shrimp boats up and down the west coast from Bremen to Husum. Then one day by chance he caught sight of the cottage beyond the dyke. And deep down something stirred and a name emerged on the tip of his tongue: Carl.

The man talks for over an hour. And the longer he talks, the more he knows, knows in his heart of hearts, that this woman who has just served him tea in a delicate china cup is his mother. It's the way her glance feels on his skin. He has experienced that very same glance, from those very same eyes, before – a long, long time ago. His skin is recognizing the glance of his mother. And maybe that's why he's talking so much. Because when he stops she will withdraw her glance from him. Maybe for ever. And there is nothing the man can do about that.

While he talks, Anna doesn't once take her eyes off him. His gaze is directed slightly towards the left, towards the trees. At the beginning Anna's attention unsettles him, she can sense it. But then he calms down. A couple of times she nods to encourage him to go on. His story rings true and eerily could belong to her Carl. But this man in front of her is so unlike Carl – they couldn't be more different. Even if Carl had suffered all that this man in front of her has suffered, could he have changed that much? It isn't just the way he looks. Maybe this man is even as young as he claims, in his early thirties.

A tough life leaves its marks after all. But could his nature have changed so much? This man is simple and slow-witted. Carl had been given more than his fair share of talents. He was musical, artistic, sporty. Whenever he applied his mind, he learned fast. She still remembers how easily Carl picked up languages. He did English and Latin at school. This man says he couldn't even speak any other language when he woke up on the other side. Can talent and energy change or even disappear with memory? Your nature surely doesn't change with your ability to remember?

The man has stopped talking. He's still looking out towards the trees. Suddenly Anna leans forward – she's not following a rational decision, she's acting on instinct. She lifts her flat hand. The man flinches, ducks.

'No, no,' she soothes him, understanding that he is misinterpreting her action. 'I just want to touch your head.'

She wants to see if her hand will recognize the head of her baby. Whenever she strokes Trine's head, a current of recognition shoots through her body: it's her baby's head that she's holding in her hand, the shape of her hand and the shape of the head are the same when they first make contact. Her hand recognizes her baby.

The man now holds still, very still. He's hunched forward, his head slightly askew, his fingers clawed around the metal armrests of the garden chair, ready to jump, ready to run. He's holding his breath too, watching from the corner of his eye as Anna's hand descends onto the top of his head. Why is she doing this? Is she pitying him? Or has she suddenly realized that he's telling the truth, that he is Carl?

And at that thought his body relaxes. And a relief that he can't remember ever feeling, but as it washes through him he understands he's been seeking for the last twelve years, takes hold of him and rocks him gently. And he closes his eyes and he feels Anna's hand, his mother's hand, travelling down the back of his head.

A few years ago her shed began to overflow: she could hardly step into it any longer. Now she keeps all the glass - the shards and the bottles and the jars - in her bedroom, on shelves that run from floor to ceiling along all four walls, shelves that she built from planks and washed-up pieces of timber she has found. Often she lies on her bed and watches the rays of the evening sun stroke their way across the shiny multicoloured surfaces - red and green and brown and blue and see-through glass. But it was only when Trine set fire to the shipwreck and it nearly burned, saved simply by a stroke of luck or a change of wind direction, that Anna was suddenly able to visualize how to assemble what she'd been collecting. She has always felt, since Carl's death, that collecting flotsam and jetsam was no senseless undertaking, no hoarding of junk and rubbish; that eventually an image would come to her, an image that would reveal how to assemble the pieces.

The man is now semi-conscious. He's leaning heavily on her. He has put his arm around her shoulder and Anna is able to hold him around his waist. She helps him up the stairs and into her room. He falls onto the bed and she covers him with her duvet. She puts on some clothes. In the kitchen she fills four hot-water bottles, then tucks them around him. She lights the fire in her bedroom and rekindles the fire downstairs.

For a moment she stands in front of the sleeping man. His lips are blue, his breathing regular. She lays her flat hand on his chest to see if he will wake up. He doesn't.

She sits down on the bed. She doesn't even know what colour his eyes are. Gently her fingertips descend on his forehead. It's like touching ice. She fetches Trine's duvet and puts it over him too. Then she crouches at the end of the bed, leaning with her back against the iron frame. She lifts the covers and takes one foot between her thighs while she begins to massage the other. After a while she changes foot. She feels his blood beginning to circulate again. But his cheeks remain pale. He doesn't stir.

Once again she changes the hot-water bottles. Two at a time, so as not to leave him without some source of heat. His body still oozes coldness. She feels his pants underneath the duvet. Still damp. She pulls them down, drops them onto the floor. Then she pushes her hands back underneath the cover and carefully lets them travel over his upper body while scrutinizing his face. She'd be ashamed if he were aware that a strange woman was running her hands over his body. With flat palms, she draws little circles across one arm, then the other, then one leg, then the other. His blood is quivering now, but the coldness remains deep in his bones. She puts the guard in front of the fire and leaves the bedside lamp burning, in case he wakes up. She kisses him on his cold forehead, then closes the door quietly.

After a while she comes back. She shouldn't leave him alone. What if he needs her help when he awakes? She pulls the armchair away from the fire and closer to the bed. She will watch over him.

ANNA STILL REMEMBERS lying with him one summer - the summer he turned three - at almost every low tide possible, on their tummies for hours in the mud waiting for the lugworms to appear. Carl was scared of stepping on lugworm casts because he thought that they were the worms and if he stepped on them he would kill them. So Anna wanted to show her son how these casts came about - that they are merely lugworm poo and the worms have buried themselves underneath in the mud once again.

OTTO, THE SEA captain, had started courting Anna, the East Prussian beauty from Königsberg, when she was fifteen. Otto was nineteen years older. But handsome, imposing. Cornflower-blue eyes, dark chestnut hair and standing nearly two metres tall. Anna's friend Lisbeth got the giggles when Anna confessed that she was in love with Captain von Kollwitz, Otto von Kollwitz, who had fought in the Great War. He was now retired from the sea and worked in Berlin.

'I'm allowed to call him Otto.'

'He wants dirty things from you.'

'No.'

Anna shook her head vehemently. Otto wasn't like that. He had already talked to her father and said that if Anna still wanted to get engaged to him next year, when she was sixteen, he would ask for her hand in marriage.

'He likes my paintings,' Anna said proudly. 'And he said when we are engaged he will take me to Berlin to the Museum Island and we will drink *Sekt* Unter den Linden. And when we are married, if I still want to become an artist, he will send me to an art college.'

'Really?' Lisbeth had finally stopped giggling.

They both dreamed of becoming famous artists in Paris. They spent hours drinking tea with Madame Blanche, who taught art and dance at the girls' middle school. She had lots of books about painting. The girls loved Cézanne, Monet and Toulouse-Lautrec. Although Lisbeth would get the giggles – as she always did when dirty thoughts flashed through her mind – looking at Toulouse-Lautrec's naughty ladies. And then there was Camille Claudel. Madame Blanche was in awe of Camille Claudel and knew many stories about her. In fact, Madame Blanche was the same age as her, and they had met at the Académie Colarossi, where they had both studied art.

'Camille is a genius. She is better than any man. But she made one mistake. She fell in love with Rodin. And that drove her mad.'

Truly mad. Madame Blanche had even visited Camille in the psychiatric hospital – their teacher would never call it a madhouse or lunatic asylum: after all, Camille was suffering from an illness, Madame Blanche insisted, which might be cured one day. But it was looking increasingly unlikely. Camille became ill in 1906 and hadn't made any art since.

'But—' and Madame Blanche would show the girls photographs she herself had taken of Camille's work – *Sakountala, La Vague, Persée et la Gorgone*. Anna and Lisbeth had to memorize the names – 'look at this genius, at these emotions, this vision, this perfection.'

Madame Blanche would let go of the pictures, throw her hands in the air. Then she'd bow deeply, interlinking her hands in her lap, as if in prayer, before saying in hushed tones, 'If a woman wants to become an artist, she must never fall in love with another artist. The competition will destroy her. The man will destroy her the moment he realizes that she is better than him.'

The girls would wait patiently, knowing that their teacher hadn't finished her lecture on how to become a female artist.

'Find a sponsor, rich, who understands art but does not want to be an artist. Give him a child – one child only – and then pursue your career.'

Anna had begun the sentence and, after three words, Lisbeth had joined in. Now they both lay back in the grass laughing, their heads on their satchels.

'So you think you've found him?' Lisbeth said once she had caught her breath.

Anna nodded. She wanted to shout out loud, 'Yes, I have, and I love him,' but she held back. She didn't want to upset Lisbeth. Because back then it felt to Anna as if there was nothing that could prevent her from fulfilling her dream, from becoming an artist. Her own future shone brightly, while Lisbeth had been told only two weeks before by her father that at Christmas he would take her out of school and send her to a famous 'home economics' school to empty her head of her fancy artist ideas and turn her into a decent Prussian woman.

'Maybe Otto has a friend,' Anna now suggested in a secretive voice.

'Maybe.'

'I'll ask.'

There was a silence and Anna watched as a peacock butterfly settled on her big toe.

'What a pity we can't talk to Madame Blanche any more,' Lisbeth then said.

Three months ago Madame Blanche had been found dead in her apartment. Heart attack, some said. After all, she was an old spinster, would have turned sixty the next year. Others, especially the maths teacher and the science professor, mumbled about a much younger lover. 'That's why she went off to Berlin so often. That city run by vice. Just imagine, what old lady would be willing to travel frequently between Königsberg and Berlin? And her knees weren't any longer the best. Only someone who was rewarded with secret pleasures at the other end, don't you think?' The two grey heads bobbed up and down as the men chuckled. 'But eventually it happened as it had to. Did no one tell her at the beginning? Her young lover left her for a woman a third of Madame Blanche's age. Oh dear, the old girl didn't take it well and ended her life with a few tablets.' That's what Professor Mahlzahn whispered to Herr von der Hyde on the stairs of the girls' middle school.

'Yes, what a pity,' Anna now agreed with Lisbeth.

And maybe if they had been able to tell Madame Blanche about Otto everything might have turned out differently.

Anna never did ask about a friend for Lisbeth. For a while she'd meant to, but it seemed such a schoolgirl question and whenever Otto did mention anyone he always stressed that they were married. Eventually Anna forgot about it – or rather pushed it to the back of her mind. She began to see less and less of Lisbeth. When Lisbeth didn't return after the Christmas break Anna felt heavy with guilt and loss and she wrote to her, but she never got a reply.

Anna turned sixteen and finished school and married Otto. She wasn't keen on a long engagement, didn't want to wait any longer to go to Berlin, where she could study art for many hours a day and live and love like a proper woman. Her body was yearning for Otto and it was her idea to drive straight after the wedding to Otto's apartment in the capital. She had been fantasizing about the wedding night for months. So she was greatly surprised when she discovered that Frau Kunze, Otto's housekeeper, had turned the spare room into the 'young lady's bedroom', as she called it. All night Anna lay awake, waiting for Otto to come. But she didn't even hear a floorboard creak. Her husband's bedroom door remained firmly shut until the next morning.

At some point Anna must have fallen asleep, because when she woke he was already having breakfast.

'*Mein Schatz*, what would you like to do today?'

He greeted her with a smile, rose and pulled the chair out for her. Frau Kunze poured coffee. The only kiss Otto had so far given his young bride had been in church, a brief, shy, dry kiss. Maybe he didn't want to pressure her? He was such a gentleman.

'The entire week belongs to you,' he announced. 'And at the weekend we will drive to the North Sea, where I will show you my - no, our - cottage. It is the ideal retreat for an artist.'

For the rest of the week he didn't kiss her, and even at the cottage, where they were on their own, he prepared his bed on the sofa. Anna was at a loss. It was not what she had imagined. Even though everything else was wonderful.

What she encountered at the North Sea coast was a magnificent artwork. At low tide the black, glittering mudflats stretched as far as the eye could see. They were beautifully patterned with exposed sandbanks - some light-coloured and barren, others dark and overgrown with eelgrass - and cut across by long winding channels and gullies. And at the shore the land was intersected by hundreds of creeks. It was impossible to imagine that in just a few hours all of this would be covered by the sea, which seemed to have disappeared beyond the horizon, dropped off the face of the earth. Anna squinted, screwed up her eyes, but she couldn't see it. Yet soon it would come rushing back at an unstoppable speed, swallowing up everything in its path.

Anna wanted to own this landscape, this Wattenmeer, make it hers, feel it inside her, be in it, be part of it. And so the next day, for the first time, she walked there for hours. In some places it was so muddy that she sank thigh deep. Elsewhere it was sandy and exposed to the wind and waves, producing dizzying patterns if she stared too long.

The next time they came back to the cottage, she discovered that the landscape had changed. And that it would continue changing for ever. That the water channels altered their course or disappeared altogether, that sandbanks and mudflats changed their shapes and that salt marshes emerged or got washed away. Anna loved it.

Back in Berlin, Otto encouraged Anna to sign up at a private art college to do a foundation course. In the evenings he often worked late and so he was keen for her to go out with her fellow students. One night she came home drunk. She had been tipsy before but never drunk. His bedroom was closed, so she knew he was in. She didn't turn on the lights. She undressed in the hallway, stripping completely, then walked into his room. She wasn't sure if he stirred but she didn't stop, she didn't give him a chance. She pulled away his duvet and quickly realized that he was lying on his back, which suited her well. She noticed his upper body lifting, he might even have said something - maybe her name - and she pushed him back. At the same time, with the other hand, she pulled up his long nightshirt and sat astride him.

'Finally,' he whispered. 'I was waiting for you.'

In the next few weeks, whenever she came to his room they made love. He was a careful, attentive lover, preferring to let his young bride dictate the rhythm while she sat astride him.

Once she tried to turn on the lights – she wanted to see him – but he switched them off again, said he preferred making love in the dark. Another time they both came home merry from a night out. She began kissing him in the corridor, sliding her hand down his trousers. He gently pushed her away and asked her to wait, then went into his bedroom and closed the door. A couple of minutes later he called her. He was lying in bed under the duvet with the lights out, ready for her.

He never made the first move or attempted to kiss her. But by now she was used to it. She got what she wanted as long as she took the initiative and accepted that whatever happened between them happened in the dark in his bed without words. They had been married for nearly a year when Anna became pregnant. That was the first time he sent her away.

'I don't want to hurt the baby,' he explained.

After Carl was born, Otto said that he was happy to wait until Anna stopped breastfeeding. She didn't mind. She loved falling asleep with the baby sucking her nipple. And for a while she couldn't imagine ever feeling sexual urges again. Every inch of her appeared to be fulfilled with the little warm body beside her.

At some point she did sneak back into Otto's bedroom. Because she felt that this was what a wife should do. It took less than a couple of minutes. She was worried that the baby would wake up. And she did feel as if Otto was performing a duty.

And so the years moved on. When the war broke out Otto insisted that Anna and Carl move permanently to their cottage beyond the North Sea dyke. He thought it would be safer there than in Berlin. And he was right. So far north on the west coast, there was nothing for the enemy to bomb. Carl attended the boys' school in the nearby harbour town.

There was only one problem. The boy was scared of water. Since his birth he had spent every summer by the coast and his parents had attempted many times to teach him how to swim, year after year. But to no avail.

'I can't see my legs and my arms when they are underwater. And I'm scared they will kick a fish or some other creature,' he had explained as soon as he was old enough to put his fear into words.

'They will swim away from you, honey.' Anna tried to soothe.

Carl only shook his head and said, 'Not everything that lives in the sea can swim away. For example, seaweed. That's alive too.'

'Seaweed is a plant.'

Again he shook his head. 'My teacher says it is an animal. And he showed me a book that says so too.'

There was no way anyone could change his mind. Dr Krohn was the cleverest person he had ever known - and probably in the whole wide world - and Carl would never dare to contradict him. Dr Krohn always knew best. And yes, Carl loved his mum and dad, but they weren't as clever as Dr Krohn. They didn't know everything.

The war dragged on and Otto bought a cow and three chickens.

'It might still take a while,' he said.

The summer after Carl was born, Otto had surprised his wife by converting the old derelict barn adjacent to the cottage into an artist's studio. A wooden floor had been put down and a small stove for heat and to brew coffee on installed. The two windows on the west and east sides, the front and the back, had been enlarged and wooden shutters fixed, to be closed when the early autumn storms began to howl. Now he had a second, smaller barn built for the animals.

At first, when she was not looking after the vegetable garden or the animals, Anna continued painting. But she had painted the sea and the sky and the wind and the clouds and the horizon many times. Even now Otto still sold her paintings to business colleagues and sometimes gave them away to influential people. Her pictures looked pretty as postcards. After the foundation course at the art college she had specialized in landscape painting. Oils and watercolours. She had been a good student, diligent and attentive and with enough talent to do what was asked of her. Of course it had been enough to impress Otto's business acquaintances. The arty young wife. But Anna knew she hadn't come even close to capturing the emotions that she felt inhabited the landscape and life. The more she painted, the more she appeared to stand outside – outside the ever-changing flow of life in all its violent, gentle, ferocious, calm, beautiful, ugly aspects, which she yearned to abandon herself to. She sat at the kitchen table, the wind lashing against the windows, with dirt from gardening under her fingernails and the smell of cows and chickens under her skin. She was bored with her pretty landscape pictures.

And she felt lonely.

The kitchen was dark, even when the sun was shining outside. The heavy beams were low and oppressive.

Yes, maybe Anna could blame it all on the lack of light in the kitchen and the oppressive beams. She sighed and poured herself another cognac. She had started drinking a cognac or two in the evenings. She clinked glasses with the dust motes dancing above the table. Overhead she heard the enemy bombers flying towards the big cities.

THE MATTRESS IS heavy. Heavier than the man in her dream last night.

When Anna woke up, the stranger had gone. Her bed looked as if no one had slept in it. Outside there was no snow.

Downstairs on the kitchen table she found a note from Trine: 'Didn't want to wake you. You were fast asleep in the chair in your room. Why the chair, Mum?!? I'll see you after school.'

Anna pulls Carl's old mattress down the stairs and out to the back. Her fingers hurt. It's hard to grip.

AS OTHER WOMEN lunch or shop, Anna would now catch the train to Hamburg once a week. It was rumoured that the bombing of the big harbour city was imminent. But Anna didn't believe it would happen in broad daylight. And she always made sure that she caught the three o'clock train back. On those days, she arranged with Irene, the girl who came to help her with the vegetable garden and the animals, to provide lunch for Carl. She told them that she had to go to Hamburg to meet artists and potential buyers, and occasionally she took her portfolio with her to keep up appearances. But truth to tell, she had by now stopped painting altogether.

In Hamburg Anna would visit a hairdresser. In her bag she carried a red evening dress, lacy black underwear and high-heeled shoes. She changed in the toilets in one of the department stores, where she also put on make-up and earrings. Then she hailed a cab and asked the driver to stop at the top end of the narrow street.

Each time it was the same room, out at the back on the third floor. The rooms were impeccable and therefore not cheap. After all, cleaners had to work by the hour, ensuring a quick, spotless turn-around. Anna had an arrangement with Fräulein Lola at the reception. For an extra Mark she could leave her bag with the everyday clothes in behind the counter. That was important to Anna. She couldn't see herself walking up the three narrow flights with a big bag over her shoulder. Instead she wanted to swing her handbag on its golden chain.

In the room there was a simple wooden double bed with a narrow wardrobe in the corner. Wooden bedside tables with red lampshades. French doors with wooden shutters out onto a tiny balcony. A pink carpet next to the bed. An en suite bathroom, unusual for such an establishment.

Sometimes she lay down on the bed, dressed or naked or wearing only her bra and knickers. But always the high heels on her feet. Sometimes she wouldn't lie down at all, just waited for him by the door. Or he would wait for her by the door. Against the wall. They never talked. Never lay in each other's arms afterwards. That's not what she paid for.

The men in Anna's room were always good-looking, impeccably clean and smooth-shaven. Young. Her age, not Otto's. And occasionally she did wonder how they had so far managed to avoid the war. But it was none of her business and, actually, she didn't really care.

She changed back into her normal clothes in the small cloakroom by the reception. Fräulein Lola never raised an eyebrow or asked any questions. In Fräulein Lola's world, Anna's behaviour was really not very remarkable.

But there was one time when things went differently.

It was she who sat down at his table in the small, dark cellar bar.

'May I?'

He nodded. He had an empty beer glass in front of him. Now he ordered another, a small one because it was only one o'clock in the afternoon and he had to head back to his desk. He asked if she would like a drink too. She requested a cognac. Every now and then they exchanged the odd sentence. They had more to drink. As they left the bar just after two, again she was the one who pulled him into a doorway and kissed him. She put her finger on his lips after they let go of each other. She led him along the pavement. Eventually they entered the narrow door of the hotel and walked into the lobby, which was painted dark red, with the concierge, Fräulein Lola, sitting behind an old bar converted into a reception desk. The man – yes, because Fräulein Lola was a man, even though he wore thick eyeliner and red lipstick and his short cropped hair was dyed blonde and he wore a lady's silk blouse, the first three buttons open to reveal thick black chest hair – handed Anna the key, barely looking up from his book. Fräulein Lola knew Anna very well, of course.

Afterwards the man was lying on his side, watching her get out of bed, watching her back, her behind, her well-formed thighs, her muscular calves, her beautiful ankles. She shuffled over to the door and disappeared inside the bathroom. When she came back into the room, a whiff of fresh soap entered with her. Her hair was pinned up. She had washed off her make-up. She briefly smiled at him. Then she began to dress herself. He watched her from the bed.

'How much do I owe you?'

She didn't react. She put on her suspender belt, picked up one stocking, placed her right foot on the armchair. She was turned to the side. He was able to see her profile. Her breathing was regular, her mouth slightly open, her eyes concentrated on her fingers as they picked up a stocking. She bent her knee and slowly slipped the stocking over her toes, then unrolled it. Upwards. Millimetre by millimetre.

They hadn't spoken since leaving the bar. Anna liked it that way. Words run the risk of getting in the way, distracting from the fantasy. Anna also liked it that he thought she might want payment. She had never before picked up someone from the bar. They were less clean-shaven, more real than the men she would order downstairs from Fräulein Lola.

Anna clipped her stocking to the suspender belt, switched to the other foot. Fastened the second stocking to the belt. Put on the dress, the high heels.

She stood at the end of the bed. She liked him, liked him for his muscular, manly, middle-aged body. In all honesty, she preferred them older, like him. And he possessed a concentration, a determination that made him appear rigid at times. She liked that too. She tucked up her dress just enough to pull down her knickers. Then she moved onto the bed and on top of him.

Afterwards she kissed him again, before she rolled off him and the bed. She pulled down her dress, picked up her knickers and her bag, and stuffed her underwear inside, then opened the door and was gone. He didn't even have time to ask if they were going to see each other again. She imagined him listening to her as she disappeared along the corridor, wondering if her step was light and her hips were swinging, but he was no judge of a woman's walk, she could tell.

At the reception desk the man pushed the key towards the blonde creature, who extended a hand with long, red-painted nails.

'How much is the room?'

Red-painted lips parted and a very deep voice said, 'All paid for, darling.'

'Does the lady come here often?'

'Occasionally.'

The man didn't know what to make of the answer. Maybe he'd asked the wrong question. What he wanted to know was if she brought other men here, and if this was, well, her line of work. He shook his head. No, he didn't actually want to know that either. He wanted to know if he could see her again. Here. That and only that was what he wanted to know. Nothing else.

'She left a note for you.' Fräulein Lola handed the man a little folded slip of paper. 'She said only to give it to you if you asked after her.'

Anna and the man met again at the bar the following week, had a couple of drinks, went back to the hotel.

Two weeks later, when she arrived for their fourth rendezvous, Anna saw Gestapo outside the bar. Without stopping, she walked straight past and went to the hotel, paid without using the room and took her bag. That day Anna caught the two o'clock train out of Hamburg.

After their first afternoon together, she and the man had never exchanged another word.

Anna liked it that way.

ANNA IS SAWING and drilling and hammering and nailing out by the shipwreck. Sometimes she lifts her head and observes Trine and Hauke walking hand in hand in the distance. Her daughter has abandoned the ship, hasn't even asked what her mother is doing here.

Anna installs the horizontal beams and props them up with planks. Then she begins thinking about moving the pieces of glass from her bedroom out to the wreck. She doesn't want any breakages. It feels important that she should return them to the sea in the same condition they were handed to her in the first place.

Anna cycles into town and buys all the newspapers and magazines she can find. Then she wraps each glass item carefully and carries them in her rucksack and two wicker baskets - one in each hand - to the wreck. Eventually she stops counting how often she goes back and forth. She has accumulated a lot over the years.

'YOU ARE NOT signing up. Not now. The war will be finished soon.'

'And so you think we should just hand over the country to the enemy?'

'They might be our saviours,' she whispered.

This was something one shouldn't say out loud. Even now.

'You don't know what you are talking about!' Carl's voice boomed through the kitchen and jumped off the walls.

Anna was standing by the stove. Her son was sitting at the table.

'Don't talk to me like that. I'm your mother,' she hissed.

The wooden chair behind her scraped along the stone floor. Involuntarily her left eye flinched. She didn't like to notice her fright. Didn't like to be scared of Carl, her own son. He had overtaken her in height more than a year ago. He was now about two heads taller than his mother and towered over most of his classmates. But while until the previous summer he had been as thin as a beanstalk, now he had filled out. Every morning at five, Anna heard him working out, push-ups, pull-ups, hack squats, lifting the weights that his father had bought him for his last birthday.

So far Carl had never laid a hand on his mother. But he had started to use his physical strength and superiority to intimidate her. Especially when he was cross with her. When he felt that she was holding him back. That she was still treating him like a little boy, a son, and not the man he thought he had already become.

Anna heard him walking around the table, towards her. She steadied herself by gripping the wooden spoon more tightly, wishing at the same time that she hadn't, that she didn't feel the need to do it. He was her son. He would never hit her. Otto had never hit her.

Carl was now standing right next to his mother, turned towards her. His chest pushed out, touching her left arm, his face pointed downwards, staring at the top of her head, his breath moving her hair.

'I'm going to fight for our country.'

An ice-cold draught entered the kitchen as Carl opened the back door. Then it shut with a bang. For a moment longer Anna's eyes held the wooden spoon still hovering a few centimetres over the frying pan, not even blinking, waiting for something else to happen. But there was nothing. The shaken walls of the old cottage had settled back into themselves.

She took the pan from the hob but didn't extinguish the flame. She liked the glow and the extra heat. Only then did it strike her that Carl must have gone out barefoot. He had come into the kitchen not wearing socks or his house shoes.

'My socks are wet and my slippers are too small,' he had grumbled when she had told him off. The stone floor was ice cold.

'Then wear Father's.'

He had thrown himself at the seat by the table and gulped down his glass of milk. For a second she had wondered if she should go and fetch him another pair of socks. But by the time she came back down he would probably have gone to do his homework or, more likely, headed outside for his early-evening workout. And she wanted him to at least eat something. She was increasingly losing control over her son, but if there was one thing she was still able to do then that was to feed him. And that made her feel useful.

And less guilty.

The first horrible clash they had had was a year ago, when her pregnancy started showing. Carl was skiving off school more and more and Anna didn't know where he went instead.

'None of your business,' he answered back when she confronted him. 'And anyway, you can't talk,' he added with a disgusted glance towards her belly.

She was taken aback, didn't know how to reply. Up to that moment she hadn't expected her son to guess or even doubt that Otto was the father of the sibling she was carrying. Otto knew of course. She hadn't been in his bed since the Führer had come to power. When she had told her husband about her pregnancy, he had stipulated only one condition: 'I'm the father.'

Now Anna said to her son, 'Go to your father and mention your suspicion to him. I wonder how he will react.'

Maybe she shouldn't have said it. Maybe her loyalty should have been with her son in that moment, not with her husband. Maybe Otto would have been able to handle the breaking of a promise better than her son the lie.

She would have loved to put her arms around Carl.

He had already turned away.

Now Anna walked across the kitchen and peeped into the small corridor. There were Carl's boots and his socks. She bent down to pick them up. Only they were both bone-dry. She left them and straightened up again. Pain shot through her lower back. She leaned against the doorframe, closing her eyes. Stars shone brightly behind her closed lids.

Carl must have walked barefoot across the marshes coming back from school, carrying his boots and socks. Anna thought he had stopped that nonsense. When she had first noticed it, just before the autumn break, she'd assumed he was taking off his boots to save the lugworms once again, as he used to do when he was a small child. A wave of glowing love for her son had risen inside her. Deep down he was still the sensitive, considerate boy who would not even dare to step on the coiled worm casts at low tide for fear of killing the animals.

But this time he had just laughed, laughed at her and himself as a small boy.

'It's so that I toughen up, in preparation for the war. Russia is a cold country after all.'

ANNA HAD NO idea how Otto could protect Carl, if he could do something that would mean Carl wouldn't be drafted, wouldn't be sent to the front. But she wrote a tearful letter to Berlin asking her husband to try. To see if there might be a way. And Otto found a way.

A couple of weeks after the letter, the mayor of the nearby town summoned Anna to his office.

'We have to erect a new camp not far from here,' he announced. 'It was supposed to be built closer to the Danish border, but thanks to your husband, Frau von Kollwitz, who persuaded Berlin that near here there is a far more pressing need as the dykes have to be strengthened, it will now be erected in the forest just outside town.' The mayor had a twinkle in his eye, like a naughty little boy. 'The SS needs back-up at nights and our boys have been selected to help.'

FROM THE BEGINNING there was the odd gunshot coming from the direction of the new labour camp in the forest just outside town. Anna never heard it because their cottage was too far away. But on Saturdays in town others talked about it. And everyone knew that Carl and his two friends – the mayor's Helmut and the doctor's Erwin – were now employed as auxiliary guards at the camp. That's why Frau Schmidt, the butcher's wife, was always eager to share the latest news about the camp with Anna.

'Some trouble there again last night. Heard a couple of shots. The poor boys, so brave, and such responsibility. Hope your Carl is OK.'

She added an extra sausage. Anna understood the gesture. The woman was hoping for more gossip, so that she had something exciting to pass on to her next customers. But even if Anna had wanted to, she had nothing to tell.

'Thank you for your concern, Frau Schmidt. But the camp is well organized. They've got everything under control. The shots you might have heard are only the occasional warnings. We don't need to fear anything.'

'Oh, I'm so relieved to hear that. And please . . .'

And now Edda Schmidt added yet another sausage, this time because she suddenly realized that her desire for gossip could be misconstrued in such a way that she might be thought to be doubting the organization and safety measures at the labour camp. Not only could such suspicion, if it started to spread, cost her the family's trading licence, but also there was nothing further from her mind than distrusting the Führer and his men. In this town her dear Wolfgang had been the first to join the Party and ever since they had included the Führer in their prayers – morning, noon and night.

'And please,' she now continued, 'Frau von Kollwitz, I just want to stress that since the camp has been set up I feel much safer because so many more trustworthy men are close by. The SS guards are our regular customers. I prepare them their lunches on their days off. What delightful and good-mannered young men. No, my enquiry regarding your son was merely in the spirit of heartfelt admiration. I wish I had a son like him. But God only gave me five daughters.'

Edda Schmidt let go of the knife on the counter and briefly touched the Mother's Cross she only ever took off in the bath and at night. It was bronze. She had hoped for silver but after the fifth child her Wolfgang was spent. He was a good man but lacked vigour. Anyway, Edda Schmidt had now observed how Anna von Kollwitz's eyes followed her hand as it moved to the cross. Probably against her will, because she averted her glance again straight away, pretending it never had happened. But Edda Schmidt had noticed. With satisfaction. It had put the von Kollwitz woman back in her place. Her husband might be someone important in Berlin and her son might now be guarding the enemy in the camp, but she, Edda Schmidt, only a simple woman, who'd never been south of the Elbe, she was the proud bearer of a Mother's Cross.

What Edda Schmidt didn't know was that Anna von Kollwitz had nothing to tell, even if she had wanted to. Except that she was pleased her son would not be drafted and instead had a job close to home where his life wasn't at risk. These labour camps were well organized, guarding the country's prisoners of war with respect and dignity, as she'd been assured by Otto and others. But Anna would never whisper a word of her relief to anyone. Envious tongues could easily misinterpret it as a lack of commitment to the inevitable victory of the Fatherland.

But needless to say, the odd gunshots Edda Schmidt intermittently mentioned troubled Anna. What if the labourers weren't as well behaved as Otto had led her to believe? What if the guards weren't as in control as Otto had assured her they were? What if they were up against a challenge here that they had never been trained for? Could Carl and his friends be in danger?

Anna woke in the middle of the night in a cold sweat. Had she heard a gunshot? She held her breath. Nothing. She was too far away. Leaden silence surrounded her. And the knowledge that this silence could not be pierced by any noise from the camp was almost unbearable and she wished she was living right next to it so that she could be aware of everything.

'HOW WAS LAST night?' Anna asked.

For the last five minutes Carl had been scrubbing his hands under the kitchen tap. Anna could see even from where she was standing, near the larder cupboard, that they'd turned bright red and the back of his left hand had started bleeding. From the scrubbing. Where the skin had worn thin. The excessive cleaning habit had started a couple of weeks ago.

'Fine,' came her son's monosyllabic answer.

Anna opened the cupboard door even though she had just closed it. She busied herself with moving things along the shelves. Any excuse to remain in the kitchen and maybe exchange a few words with her son. Once Carl had eaten his breakfast he'd be heading straight to school.

'People mentioned shooting from the camp the other night again?' It had started off as a statement but then she decided it might sound less concerned if she made it into a question.

'Don't know what they're talking about.'

There was no way of getting through to her son.

'You'd tell me if you were in danger, wouldn't you?'

She had opened the little sack of sugar, their last, and looked inside. Now she was closing it again. Keeping busy. Very busy. And just casually chatting with her son.

'You'd be the first to know.' The sarcasm was palpable in his voice.

Then suddenly, as if Carl realized he had gone too far and upset his mother more than he'd intended, he stood next to her, stooped down and planted a kiss on top of her head.

'Don't worry about me, *Mutti*. I'm fine.'

Anna held on to that sentence like a piece of driftwood, hoping that it would prevent her from drowning.

ANNA'S ON HER knees inside the burnt-out ship's carcass. In her right hand she's holding the big kitchen knife. She lifts it above her head, then brings it down into the soft mattress. In a straight line, she cuts the mattress open, tears out the stuffing, then replaces it with the small rocks she has brought with her. She returns as much stuffing as possible. Bent over, she mends the tear with tight stitches. With the stones inside, the mattress – Carl's old mattress – will sink to the bottom of the sea.

'HERE, IT'S YOUR night tonight.' The SS guards pushed their rifles into the hands of the three boys. 'And no word to anyone. We'll be back in a few hours.'

The SS guards, only a couple of years older than the boys, had already turned their backs, when one looked over his shoulder. 'And don't shit your pants, lads. Remember you've got the guns. And this evening the prisoners are docile. We've exhausted them during the day.'

The prisoners had been reinforcing the dyke. But their work was shoddy and far too slow. The only thing that kept them going was the whip. The guards had had a lot of bother with them today. They deserved their fun tonight.

The door slammed shut. For a moment the three boys – Carl, Erwin and Helmut – didn't move. They couldn't believe their luck, each silently wondering if at any moment the door might swing open once again and the SS guards, all six of them, march back in, bent over double because they had played such a good joke on those three sissies who still, at the age of seventeen, attended school rather than defending the Fatherland, or at least earned their money in an honest, manly way. The guards couldn't stand these boys. Twice a week they had to babysit them because the camp's commanding officer knew the commanding officer of Neuengamme camp, of which this was an outpost, and that officer was best friends with the father of one of the boys, a big shot in Berlin, or something like that. By sending the boys here under the pretext that they were needed, doing a valuable job, the army couldn't draft them. It was a bloody rotten game, all six SS guards agreed. So tonight, after such a hard day, it was payback time for the boys. For once they could get at least a glimpse of what it felt like to guard these stinking creatures in the middle of a dark forest all night long.

The clock on the table was ticking. Tick-tock. Tick-tock. Tick-tock. But the door remained shut. The guards had gone.

Carl threw himself into the chair behind the desk.

'Wow! Can you believe it? We are in charge.'

He banged his feet up onto the desk and cradled the gun in his arms like a baby, running his right hand over it gently.

Helmut lifted his gun and aimed at the wastepaper basket in the corner. Erwin had walked over to the window and was peeking through the curtains.

'Do you think they know it's just us tonight?'

'Who?' Helmut asked, pretending to shoot the wastepaper basket. '*Peng, peng.*'

'Well, them over there.' Erwin pointed with a movement of his head to the barracks.

Carl shrugged. 'Who cares? We know what to do, don't we?'

They took it in turns. Two of them made the rounds outside every fifteen minutes. For the first couple of hours it felt thrilling. Then they started to get tired.

'I could do with more than fifteen minutes' break in here,' Helmut said, yawning as Carl and Erwin walked back in. It was now Erwin's turn to remain in the warmth. 'Or else something needs to happen to keep me awake,' Helmut added.

They had witnessed the guards waking up the prisoners in the middle of the night, to teach them a lesson, to remind them who was boss.

'Let's not.' Erwin guessed what his friend was hinting at. 'I'd prefer to get through this night without any trouble.'

'But if the guards come back and realize that we had everything under control simply because there was an *absence—*' Helmut stressed the word deliberately – 'of trouble, they will continue to look at us as sissies. If we want to show them that we are their equals and shut them up for ever, this is our chance. We need to create a bit of excitement, just enough so it looks as if we had to work to keep the peace. That'll impress them. You heard them, they think nothing will happen tonight. That's why they left us in charge.' Then he added, 'We're sober, boys. This kind of thing only ever gets out of control when everyone is drunk.'

There was something in what Helmut was saying that appealed to Carl. After all, they were here because of his dad, and the longer they remained here, the more it was clear to the three friends that they had been fobbed off by Carl's dad. The boys had wanted to join the army. Everyone around them was being drafted. Wasn't that what they had hoped for ever since they were able to walk? They were six years old when Hitler came to power and their parents had signed them up for the HJ. That's where they'd met, at the HJ summer camp, became best friends on the first day.

It was around the time they had decided not to wait any longer but to sign up themselves instead that, completely unannounced, Carl's dad arrived from Berlin. His massive frame filled the sitting room. He had summoned all three boys.

'The SS guards need back-up at the camp. I put your names forward. It's an honour to serve the Fatherland in such a way. Don't disappoint me, boys.'

At first the three friends were thrilled. They thought they had struck lucky and been given a post with responsibilities far beyond being a common soldier in the army, based on their courage, prowess and strength. They believed they had been chosen. By the Fatherland. By the nation. By the race. And not, as it turned out, by Carl's father, who wanted to protect them from getting killed, and was thus preventing them from ever becoming part of the victory they had been taught to believe in since they were six years old. A victory that was surely imminent.

Now Carl, Erwin and Helmut were excluded from this victory. They were not necessary in this camp. They were a laughing stock. And they felt like fools. Fools in the eyes of the SS guards. Fools in the eyes of the boys they once knew and who had by now become heroes, more often dead than alive. And worst of all, fools in the eyes of each other.

Something had to happen. Helmut was right. If the world wasn't offering them a chance to prove themselves as men, then they had to create their own opportunities.

They walked into the barracks, turned on the lights and shouted at the men to line up outside.

There were six barracks with thirty men in each. No women or children. Russians and Poles. POWs all. The last scum that got sent to these outposts.

The four watchtowers had woken from their slumber. Excitement in the yard. They shone their floodlights.

The show could begin.

The prisoners had to take off their clothes. Snow was now falling heavily. The first flakes had descended half an hour ago when the boys were still discussing what to do. A sign from heaven. Let them stand in the snow naked. That'd show them.

And there they stood naked. Shivering. Some were even swaying.

'*Still gestanden*,' Helmut shouted.

The ranks stopped swaying. But there! Someone folded in the front row. It was in Carl's section. For a second Carl hesitated, caught Helmut's eye – and Helmut jerked his head with the unspoken challenge for Carl to do something, to bring his prisoner back into line. Carl rushed forward and rammed his boot into the bundle on the floor.

'Get up!'

The man attempted to raise himself. His neighbour helped him up, then supported him. Carl was inclined to let this pass. Good enough. He turned and walked back to stand in line with Helmut and Erwin. He noticed how quiet the yard was, only the crunching of the snow underneath his boots roared in his ears.

'He's down again,' Helmut said as soon as Carl had come to a halt. 'Get that shit under control,' he then hissed. 'You owe us, mate. Your father has got us into this, you'll get us out. Won't he, Erwin?'

Erwin nodded but avoided looking either of his friends in the eye.

Carl wished he'd drunk some schnapps. Alcohol made this sort of thing easier. He'd once lent a hand to one of the guards to sort out a prisoner. After each kick the guard and he stopped to take a gulp from the bottle.

No thinking, he told himself now. What had to be done had to be done.

He watched his boot kick and kick again. Not good enough. He put more weight behind the kick. He couldn't just watch. He, Carl himself, needed to become the kick.

The bundle no longer moved. A cough took hold of Carl. He bent forward. There was a pain in his chest, he struggled to breathe. Suddenly someone grabbed his ankle.

'Please have mercy on us, sir. You are so young. Don't commit any sins that will taint your soul for ever.'

Huge hollow eyes looked at him. And then Carl realized. The words had been spoken in perfect German. Not even a hint of an accent.

ANNA FILLED THE tub with hot water. Carl cried as he sat in the bath while his mother soaped his back, his legs, his arms. He had no wounds. The boy hadn't allowed her to be so close for a long time. Anna put him to bed and kissed him goodnight on both cheeks as she used to. Then she sat in the chair by his side, watching over his breathing until it was quiet and deep.

The wind picked up, howling, and the snow turned into rain that hammered against the windowpanes. Carl developed a fever and Anna remained by his side, leaving the room only once to nurse the baby.

She knew they would eventually come looking for him. At first she assumed it would be routine, but then Carl stirred and pleaded, 'Please Mum, help me. I've done nothing wrong. Still they won't believe me, I know.'

She soothed him. 'They will just want to ask you some questions, surely.'

'No. You don't understand. They will take me away.'

She gave him hot milk that was meant for the baby and he fell back into a feverish sleep.

And then she suddenly remembered the shipwreck that had washed up only a fortnight ago. She doubted that many of the townspeople, if any, knew about it yet. No one came out here, especially not in the winter. She hesitated to send her son there. The water was coming back in. She would have liked to wait until the next low tide. She stood by the window, looking out towards the track that led into town. Everything was dark. And calm. The wind had dropped.

'Do you see, they are coming!'

Carl had appeared next to her, pointing with his finger. She stared until she too saw two headlights dancing towards them. Carl dressed and she packed a bag with their last bread and cheese.

'The water is deep just before the sandbank, remember. But you will be able to wade through. Hold the bag over your head. I will come as soon as it's light and the tide is going out.'

And she held his head between her hands and pulled it down towards her and kissed the top.

The Gestapo searched the cottage and the garden.

'You are sure, *gnädige Frau*, you haven't seen him since he left for his shift yesterday evening?'

'He hasn't come back, Officer.'

By the time the men left the wind had picked up again. Anna hoped that Carl had made it to the ship by now.

ANNA IS LYING on Carl's mattress on the floor of the shipwreck, looking up into the star-filled night sky through the empty bottles and pieces of glass that she's been collecting for years, now hanging from beams made out of driftwood that she has fixed from one side of the boat to the other. Every now and then a light breeze moves through the huge glass mobile above her and takes with it a fleeting jingle up into the dark sky and towards the stars.

She used to wonder what kind of art she might have been able to make if grief hadn't cornered her, deprived her of images, of thoughts, of language, of visions. And all that she had left to do was to roam the mudflats, collecting flotsam and jetsam. Waiting.

Anna's arms are by her side, her hands are gently stroking the mattress beneath her. She can feel the big stones.

Clouds must have moved in from the sea. No more starlight, no more moonlight is penetrating. And for a moment there is total silence. Yet the silence is deceptive. Anna senses that the night creatures in the mudflats have begun to stir: eels crawling from their hiding places, lobsters daring to venture out in search of shrimps and mussels, and catfish baring their teeth, getting ready for the kill.

Soon the sun will be rising. The sky is getting lighter now. Among all the glass – red and blue and yellow and brown and see-through – Anna has also hung shells: cockles and mussels and whelks. They will help the wind and the waves to compose on the mobile their farewell piece of music for Carl - music that will accompany the shipwreck on its last journey. She can hear the swoosh of the approaching waves. It will be a very high tide - the first in fifteen years - high enough to once again flood the sandbank. And this time the vessel will float. Because this time Anna has left nothing to chance. Her final task, after the sawing and nailing and building and hanging of glass pieces from the beams had finished, was removing the sand from around the wreck.

The sun begins to hit the glass. Anna opens her arms and her legs: a starfish inviting the shadows to play on her naked skin. She imagines that this is what it must be like underwater, when you have given up the fight to breathe, to survive. When there is no more panic. When you have surrendered. She's holding her breath, closing her eyes. Diamond stars dance in front of her eyelids. The ship creaks. The waves have reached the sandbank, crawling underneath the vessel, freeing it from its mooring.

And Anna is waiting, waiting for Carl. To touch his face one last time.

NEW BOOKS FROM SALT

JUDITH HENEGHAN
Snegurochka (978-1-78463-174-1)

CHRISTINA JAMES
Chasing Hares (978-1-78463-189-5)

BARET MAGARIAN
Melting Point (978-1-78463-197-0)

VESNA MAIN
Good Day? (978-1-78463-191-8)

ANDREW McDONNELL
The Somnambulist Cookbook (978-1-78463-199-4)

SIMON OKOTIE
After Absalon (978-1-78463-166-6)

ELEANOR REES
The Well at Winter Solstice (978-1-78463-184-0)

TREVOR MARK THOMAS
The Bothy (978-1-78463-160-4)

This book has been typeset by
SALT PUBLISHING LIMITED
using Neacademia, a font designed by Sergei Egorov for the Rosetta Type Foundry in the Czech Republic. It is manufactured using Holmen Book Cream 70gsm, a Forest Stewardship Council™ certified paper from the Hallsta Paper Mill in Sweden. It was printed and bound by Clays Limited in Bungay, Suffolk, Great Britain.

CROMER
GREAT BRITAIN
MMXIX

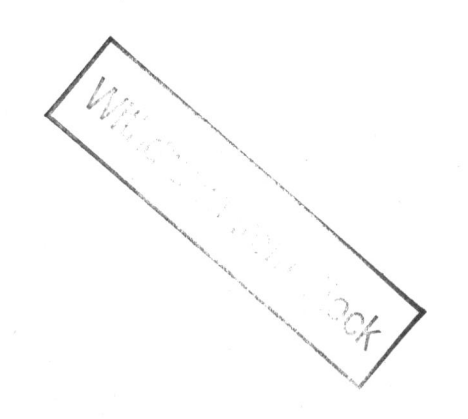